Marec Béla Steffens

THYME WILL TELL

THE ADVENTURES OF AN OLD-SCHOOL EUROPEAN HIGHWAYMAN IN HOUSTON, TEXAS

A true account
recorded by
the Tomcat Who Tells Fairy-Tales
in his sixth book
(the first one in English)

With a preface by Barrett Sills,
Principal Cellist, Houston Grand Opera

Illustrations: Krystyna Steffens

Copyright © 2014-17 Marec Béla Steffens

All rights reserved.

ISBN: 1539186598
ISBN-13: 978-1539186595

"It was a Texas solution to a Texas problem, and it worked."
James Michener, Texas

"Texas? Amo quia absurdum."
Fabulas narrans felis in imitatione Tertulliani

Proofreader: David C West, Houston TX. The usual disclaimer appliex.

For Muir and Geoff
the legendary old friends of my father's
and my Aunt Ursula's

from 🐱 and Krystyna 🐱

German version:
"Thymian in Texas" published by Geest-Verlag, Vechta 2017
www.geest-verlag.de

Author's website and contact:
www.maerchenkater.de   maerchenkater@web.de

"It was a Texas solution to a Texas problem, and it worked."
James Michener, Texas

"Texas? Amo quia absurdum."
Fabulas narrans felis in imitatione Tertulliani

Proofreader: David C West, Houston TX. The usual disclaimer appliex.

For Muir and Geoff
the legendary old friends of my father's
and my Aunt Ursula's
 from 😺 and Krystyna 😺

German version:
"Thymian in Texas" published by Geest-Verlag, Vechta 2017
www.geest-verlag.de

Author's website and contact:
www.maerchenkater.de   maerchenkater@web.de

Preface by Barrett Sills *p. 2*

Chapter the First. In which Robber Thyme feels naked *p. 5*

Chapter the Second. In which it is ascertained that reference is made to the Greyhound *p. 12*

Chapter the Third. In which the esteemed reader is being acquainted with the art of robbing a Greyhound in the proper manner, though we hope that said reader will not put such knowledge into practice *p. 16*

Chapter the Fourth. In which this account proceeds to the gates of hell, viz. a call centre *p. 24*

Chapter the Fifth. In which communication channels and a classroom training are being truefully described *p. 34*

Chapter the Sixth. In which a bank robbery is conducted in Japanese style *p. 44*

Chapter the Seventh. In which a concierge and an armadillo make their appearance *p. 54*

Chapter the Eight. One Siblinghood under God *p. 62*

Chapter the Ninth. A villa job, and other pastimes *p. 71*

Chapter the Tenth. In which the heat becomes intolerable so that abducktion becomes a much more agreeable occupation than street robbery *p. 78*

Chapter the Eleventh. In which the abducktion is being continued, until a turning point is reached *p. 87*

Chapter the Twelfth. In which, at an intersection, a stalemate occurs *p. 93*

Chapter the Thirteenth. In which, to satisfy the reader's alleged curiosity, the previous chapter is continued   *p. 105*

Chapter the Fourteenth. In which another business model is developed, and a public holiday is celebrated, though not by everyone   *p. 109*

Chapter the Fifteenth. In which the letters of the alphabet appear in a sequence never before employed in the history of literature   *p. 115*

Chapter the Sixteenth. In which the following day is described   *p. 122*

Chapter the Seventeenth. In which the superiority of the jury system is exemplified   *p. 128*

Chapter the Eighteenth. Which has no subtitle but this   *p. 135*

Chapter the Nineteenth. Which introduces us to the spiritual and the temporal lord of a gaol   *p. 146*

Chapter the Twentieth. In which we learn something important about the nature of Texas history   *p. 153*

Chapter the Twenty-First. In which we make the acquaintance of a very special township   *p. 160*

Chapter the Twenty-Second. In which Robber Thyme has a nightmare, and this true account is moving towards the end   *p. 165*

Chapter the Last. In which this true account is coming to an end   *p. 171*

The author & the illustrator   *p. 180*

PREFACE

by Barrett Sills

Principal Cellist, Houston Grand Opera, Houston, Texas

Anyone who has lived for a time abroad outside the boundaries of one's own culture understands the privilege and special insight which being an outsider affords. Many years ago I had the opportunity to do so, in Germany, where I spent my days wide-eyed and fascinated by the ongoing spectacle of life in a foreign world. The language barrier was only a small part of being an *Ausländer*.

Living daily life out of context, as it were, heightened my powers of observation and provoked thoughts and impressions that would have remained unknown to me otherwise had I stayed protected and comfortable in my native *Heimat*. As an outsider looking in, there was a sense of surreality and a sense of adventure. Being somewhat rootless and blowing in the wind inspired me. It is this feeling of inspiration which I can well imagine those from other countries and backgrounds must have also coming to Texas.

As a cellist living in Houston, I performed a recital recently which included several works in the key of E flat. As I often do, I provided spoken commentary about my ideas regarding music, and in this case in particular, the tonality of E flat. After the concert I was approached by someone who probed me further about this topic. I was quite taken by the exchange. How rare to find a concert-goer who seemingly had interest and was even fascinated by my theories on the subject of E flat! Subsequently, I learned that this gentleman, Marec Béla Steffens, had written a short story, *Das Märchen vom Es*, about the key of E flat! This was certainly the first time I had ever encountered the fantastical idea of a living and walking E flat! Little did I realize that such surreal imagination had further wild manifestations to reveal.

Like all of Texas, Houston is a place of extremes. So full of contradictions, yet often the outlandish realities of life here go hardly noticed by those of us who make this city our home. The intrinsic character of a place is often best captured through transient eyes and first impressions all too often turn out to be the most true. Houston is an environment that has fueled the imagination of many, and I would venture to say that these over-the-top attributes of Houston have rarely been captured as cleverly and trenchantly as by Marec Béla Steffens in this highly original and vastly amusing tale, *Thyme Will Tell*.

Here are kaleidoscopic impressions of a society, woven into a narrative fabric by fantasy characters who give voice to biting socialcritique in the best tradition of Jonathan Swift. The humor is multi-layered, often ambiguous, and always enjoyable, especially for those of us in situ and made aware of the irony in our everyday culture.

Very little escapes the scrutiny of the outsider looking in: gun culture, out of control litigation, political correctness run amok, to name just a few. There are so many strands of commentary about the many absurdities of contemporary life in Houston.

This is a portrayal of an overall life experience, rife with idiosyncrasies to be savored and enjoyed and from which ultimately we are saved because we are all in this together. Behind the satire lies a hidden appreciation and affection for the craziness of it all.

By nature I'm not someone to laugh out loud at something I read. Clever humor can bring a smile to my face, but in reading Thyme will Tell, I found myself giving full meaning to the word guffaw. It has been a long time since I've read a book as enjoyable, and even longer since I've read a book that has caused me to laugh out loud page after page!

An added pleasure are the sharply drawn and delightfully sardonic illustrations by Krystyna Steffens which encapsulate and prove the adage that a picture is worth a thousand words.

I'm grateful for my serendipitous encounter with Marec Béla Steffens and for his colorful account of this crazy, at times outlandish, and wonderful place I call home. I have to agree with *Tomcat Who Tells Fairy Tales:* reality so often beats absurdity. *Amo quia absurdum est…!*

CHAPTER THE FIRST

IN WHICH ROBBER THYME FEELS NAKED

Robber Thyme felt naked. For the first time since his undeserved prison term, he was without his two pistols and his three knives. And that on a business trip! But the security staff at the airport would not listen to his arguments: "What if some terrrrrrorrrists want to hijack the airrrplane, eh?" – No way. They just did not understand.

Robber Thyme felt uncomfortably naked. But the long flight was almost over, and he liked what he saw: not the desert he had expected, but green marshland. The desert indeed! At the travel agency back home in Germany, they had almost sent him there. For Thyme had coughed quite a bit, and the clerk expressed her compassion: "*Sie haben aber einen schlimmen Husten* / You really have a bad cough!" – "*Husten! Genau da will ich hin* / Houston! That's wherrre I want to go," Thyme explained. And then she had given him a ticket to – Catarrh, to the Emirate!

When Thyme had sorted out that Qatar was not his destination, she asked him which airport he preferred: the one frequented by Bush pilots, or the other for Hobby pilots?

On board the plane, when lunch was served, most passengers chose the beef option. They believed that would give them better standing with the Texas immigration officers. Rumours said that chicken and pork eaters would face an extra level of scrutiny, and vegetarians would be denied entry altogether.

And now Robber Thyme had arrived at Bush airport, waiting in the long line for immigration. He chatted a bit with his neighbour in the queue, an elderly gentleman with a grey goatee beard who had just arrived from Paris, although he certainly was neither American nor French. He carried a time-worn black leather bag with a faded tag and the label, 'Flying Dutchman', still discernible. (He did not look Dutch either, though.) Here in the air conditioning, his long coat combined with a black ten-gallon hat came in handy. Would he like to share a ride downtown with Thyme? No thanks, he was on his way to a meeting near that other airport, and would then take another flight.

Thyme's papers were first-rate: his own passport, not a stolen one, with an authentic working visa for the U.S. of A. The Robbers' Guild of his home town had arranged that with the help of their local partner organisation here. Thanks to his excellent credentials, he easily got his luggage, with pistols and knives truthfully declared as work tools, through customs. In contrast, a fellow passenger got herself into really big trouble because of a half-eaten apple in her hand.

Robber Thyme was dog-tired, but still he kept his eyes open. And very soon he observed a local colleague snatching a purse. To his surprise, Thyme saw how the pickpocket then manoeuvred a little card into the victim's pocket. "His business carrrd?" Robber Thyme wondered. (The trrrrilling r was an inheritance from his great-grandfather, the famous Robber Jaromir.)

Thyme could not resist the temptation and, although it's not cricket to steal from a colleague, pilfered one of his cards. It was not a classical business card that he got, but close enough:

> *Thank you for allowing me to steal*
> *from you. I will visit you again!*
> *Phil the Felon*

Thyme was impressed. After a while he noticed another pickpocket who would also leave a card:

> *It was a pleasure to empty your*
> *pocket! I appreciate your business.*
> *Airport Eddy*

That was certainly different from Germany with her reputation of being a service desert! It must be said, however, that not all customers duly respected these little tokens of appreciation that the U.S. pickpockets left with them. Several victims threw the cards away, or dropped them carelessly on the floor. This disregard might have been due to a certain message that all these cards carried in small print: *'Card will not be recognized as evidence in a lawsuit, be it criminal or civil.'*

Thyme admired these cards. Look at this one:

> *How was your pickpocketing
> experience with me?
> Are you 100 % satisfied?
> Call 1-800-TELL-TOM*

Other cards declared: *'We ♥ our customers!'* That was exactly why Robber Thyme had come here: to learn from the best robbers in the U.S. Although it must be said that some dissenters among Thyme's colleagues in the Robbers' Guild back home had not approved of this endeavour. They had argued with history: only the careless criminals had been deported to the colonies, so what could you expect from their descendants? But history had provided the counterargument as well: those who had managed to snatch an entire continent away from its original inhabitants could not be called unsuccessful at all.

Be that as it may, Robber Thyme felt pure bliss when he hit the hay at his hotel. At night, however, he awoke quite a few times from a noise that sounded as if people were vomiting right in front of his door. Again and again! "Sprrring brrreakers," Thyme thought. He was afraid of what he would see when he opened the door in the morning. But the carpet was spotless. And Thyme understood that the noise had been coming from the ice cube maker next to his door.

It was frightfully early in the morning. The jet-lag. Thyme decided to have a little walk in the neighbourhood, but soon he regretted this decision. Although he was reunited with his two pistols and his three knives, the kind of people he met downtown at this hour of the day made him feel rather uneasy. Was it more dangerous here to be an honest robber than his customer? Plus, the cops were casting strange looks at him. A pedestrian, how suspicious!

He walked directly back to the hotel and decided to drive straight away to the Robbers' Guild's local partner organisation. The domicile of the robbers was on Richmond Street. It looked strange – as if an architect of the German *Bauhaus* of the 1920s had been given the task of designing an air raid shelter. 'Siblinghood of Robbers,' was written above the entrance. – "Political correctness," explained the doorman-robber (whose nametag identified him as Peter) to an astonished Thyme. "We used to be called the Brotherhood of Robbers, but you can't have a name like that anymore."

While waiting for the Robber Boss, Thyme sipped a watery broth that the locals, for reasons unbeknownst to him, called coffee. Passing robbers slapped him on the shoulder. And with envious looks, or occasionally with slight signs of disapproval, they stared at Thyme's flaming red robber beard.

At last the Robber Boss was available. "Howdy! Good to see ya!" He whacked Thyme's shoulder. „How are ya?" –

Thyme set forth on an elaborate disquisition on his state and feelings on the occasion of his arrival to the New World, affected by an exhausting flight and the effects of jet-lag. But no-one was listening.

"Where are you from … Germany? That's great!" Another slap on the shoulder. "Many of us have German ancestors. This fellow over there, he's Robber Rob. He'll take care of you. I'm sure you'll have a fantastic time with us!" With that, his audience ended. Robber Thyme almost forgot to hand over the gypsum owl which was the emblem of his home town. The Robber Boss had already dived into his next telephone conference.

CHAPTER THE SECOND

IN WHICH IT IS ASCERTAINED THAT REFERENCE IS MADE TO THE GREYHOUND

First things first: Robber Rob showed Robber Thyme how to do his travel expense claim for the trip from Germany. Then he inquired what Thyme's favourite kind of job was back home, burglary? Or banking? Forget it, buddy, train robbery is totally out; we only have two trains. Two eastbound and two westbound. Per week, that is. Rob the post bus? What the heck is that? Ah, you mean the Greyhound. All right, be my guest.

Rob absolutely refused to take Thyme's rented car for the job. "A sedan? What a jalopy. Think of our reputation, buddy!" So they took Robber Rob's pickup. It took them almost an hour to get out of town. On their way they passed a cab in which the elderly gentleman was sitting whom Thyme had seen at the airport.

Robber Rob was surprised again when Thyme insisted they hide their car in the brushwood. There really was some. Thyme had imagined that he would have to be on the lookout between cacti. During the wait he passed the time with his snuff. At last the Greyhound bus came. Not as silvery and shining as Thyme knew them from the toy cars in his youth, but on his first day in the States he did not want to be picky. He adjusted his robber's hat, and with "Huzzah!" and "Horrrrrrido!" he stormed out of the brushwood and onto the highway.

Traffic was horrible. Cars swerved around Thyme left and right. One driver even slowed down and advised Robber Thyme to wear an orange vest: "Your boss has to give you one, that's the law!" he insisted.

The greyhound bus would not slow down a bit. "Hoho!" made Robber Thyme, drew his pistol and fired a warning shot in the air. A friendly wave from the driver, that's all he got. Thyme was outraged at this lack of respect for an honest robber and his gun. "Just you wait!" He fired another warning shot, right over the bus's roof. This time a few passengers waved, too.

"Thunderrr and Dorrria, what was that?" asked Robber Thyme when he had regained the safety of the brushwood. – "Try the next one, buddy," said Robber Rob, "in a few minutes it'll be here."

This time, Thyme fired warning shots until both magazines were empty. Again, the bus would not reduce speed. Again, the driver and many passengers would smile and wave.

Thyme stood there flabbergasted. More and more drivers would smile and wave at him. "Nice Colt you're wearing!"

shouted some. Others showed that they, too, had guns in their pickups. A few would even send a shot or two in the air to show their appreciation.

Humbled and clueless, Thyme asked Robber Rob for an explanation. – "You know, buddy, next time when you want to show off with those little pistols of yours, don't do it with such a billboard as your backdrop!" – Thyme had not noticed before that he was right in front of a giant billboard. 'The Biggest Gunshow in Texas,' it said.

"In twenty minutes there will be another bus," Robber Rob comforted Robber Thyme. "Now you better let me pick the spot, O.K.?"

This time, Thyme would fire at the tyre. That was the real thing. The bus stopped. "Höhöhö," made Thyme and walked towards the door. But Robber Rob shouted to call him back: "Darn! Here comes the headache man! What? The law man, got it?" With squeaking tyres, a patrol car stopped right in front of Robber Thyme. What a bad start for him in the New World!

Fortunately, Thyme was never short of excuses. "I just wanted to tell the bus drrriverrr that therrre's something wrrrong with his tyrrres," he intended to say. But the policeman here was cut from a different cloth than those back in Thyme's hometown. He did not wait for explanations: he fired at once! With bullets buzzing around him, Thyme leaped back into safety.

The boy in blue followed his routine. "You have the right to remain silent!" he shouted between his salvoes. "Whatever you say can be used against you! You have the right to have an attorney present while I'm shooting at you!"

Luckily for Thyme, Robber Rob was not squeamish either and provided cover fire for his guest. The bullets from his assault rifle made the cop dive behind his patrol car. And Rob fired back with words as well: "Protect our constitutional rights!" he shouted at the top of his lungs. "The right of the people to keep and use arms! Free shooting for free people!"

Weighing the power of Rob's arguments, the policeman decided not to follow Thyme into the brushwood. He instead escorted the Greyhound bus to the next city.

Thyme and Rob had escaped arrest, but a day was lost with no booty made. "A good buddy, this Thyme," Rob summarised to the Robber Boss that afternoon, "but for sure not the sharpest knife in the box." – "He might be forced to lead an honest life," mused the Boss, "which is not easy in this country." - "Or we'll have to send him over to Pennsylvania," wondered Robber Rob, "his methods are so 19th century. Let him rob the Amish, they still have horse carriages!"

Will Robber Thyme be a failure in America? Well, he does tell all his adventures to the Tomcat Who Tells Fairy-Tales so that his story will be known. Thyme will tell.

CHAPTER THE THIRD

IN WHICH THE ESTEEMED READER IS BEING ACQUAINTED WITH THE ART OF ROBBING A GREYHOUND IN THE PROPER MANNER, THOUGH WE HOPE THAT SAID READER WILL NOT PUT SUCH KNOWLEDGE INTO PRACTICE

In the United States, everyone deserves a second chance, a robber just as well as any other citizen. The Robber Boss decided to apply this principle to their guest from Europe. "Bus hold-ups are so 1950s. But for some reason unbeknownst to me, Robber Jack does one every now and then. He can take this Thyme with him next time."

Robber Thyme took an instant liking to Robber Jack. He had a pitch-black beard. Not a full beard though – the policy of the Siblinghood of Robbers would not allow that. But a moustache was all right.

"Always follow the dress code," explained Robber Jack. "No t-shirts. Polo shirts on casual Friday only. Otherwise dress shirts. Short sleeves O.K. No earrings. Savvy?" – "No prrroblem. Let's go!" Thyme was eager to leave for the hold-up. – "Wait for the tide, shipmate!" Robber Jack held him back. "We need to have a meeting first. I'll tell my cabin boy to shoot out the invitation e-mails double-quick, savvy?"

Cabin boy? Oh, that was Robber Jack's slang for his PA. A robber with a personal assistant! Thyme was impressed. Even more so when he saw the professional presentation that the PA had compiled for Robber Jack. There were street maps, bus timetables and even statistics what the hold-ups had yielded on average, compared to the budget. – "What's the bus drrriverrr's shoe size?" asked Robber Thyme. But his irony was lost on Robber Jack. "We must not inquire after personal details," he retorted. "No age or gender data. That would be considered unlawful discrimination. Savvy?" – Robber Thyme still had a lot to learn.

Jack gave Thyme a lift in his pick-up. Robber Rob and the PA followed in their own cars. The assistant (he had just earned his bachelor's degree: Texas Christian University) was of course not entitled to a pick-up yet, not even to a stolen one.

A couple of Hispanics were sitting on the beds of the two pick-ups. "Some unskilled worrrkerrrs to assist us, I suppose?" asked Robber Thyme. – "Workers? No," said Robber Jack. "They're independent contractors. They run their own businesses, and we give them subcontracts. You never want workers on your ship. They mean trouble: unions, strikes! In the midst of the nicest hold-up, they go on strike. And distribute leaflets to the victims!

That's why we support free enterprise." – "Savvy," remarked Robber Thyme.

Now the free entrepreneurs leaped into action. Using warning signs and traffic cones, they slowed the cars down and made them use the outer lane. "This makes it so much easier to stop the bus," explained Robber Jack. "Rob told me how you did it the other day, shipmate, in the midst of all traffic. All monsters of the seven seas! That was way too dangerous!"

Thyme knew that. He had already received a dressing down from Robber Lennart who was the Siblinghood's safety officer. Never before had Robber Thyme met a Norwegian capable of uttering that many words. Thyme had managed his escape only when he questioned how Robber Lennart, even if he may have studied in Dallas, would dare to decorate his cubicle all over with flags and apparel of the Dallas Cowpunchers. Wasn't that asking for trouble, and thus utterly unsafe, here in the homeland of the Houston True Texans, yeehaw!

Thyme had found out quickly that Dallas was anathema to any Houstonian with an ounce of self-respect. If they had friends there, they denied them, and if a visit could not be avoided, they wore sunglasses and false beards. Most Houstonians would not even say the name Dallas. They used D-town instead, or The-place-that-must-not-be-named.

Now follow this true account back to the Interstate. Lo and behold, there was the Greyhound bus. A salvo from Rob's assault rifle, and at once the bus stopped. The well-trained driver opened the door: "Hi, folks! How are you today?" – "Fine!!" shouted Rob, Jack and the PA. – "Tolerrrably well," added Robber Thyme.

Now Robber Jack would address the passengers: "Howdy y'all! How are y'all today?" – "Fine!!" was the unanimous answer, often accompanied by a broad grin. – Robber Thyme was impressed. Not that he would complain about his customers back home, but such a friendly and relaxed reaction by a crowd of robbery victims was unheard of in Germany. – "Isn't this a most beautiful day for being robbed?" continued Robber Jack. "But, no offence – we have to run you through the formalities first. Savvy?"

At a nod from Robber Jack, his PA started their usual *spiel*: "Ladies and gentlemen, a government warning. Resistance to robbery imposes a significant risk of severe damage to your health." – Robber Rob fell in: "The surgeon general warns you that attempted resistance significantly increases your risk to die as a victim of a criminal deed." – Then all three of them synchronously: "Resistance can cause a sudden and painful death!"

The passengers must have heard that plenty of times. Most of them did not bother to listen. Even when now the PA went through the bus, they hardly looked up. – "Is he now collecting theirrr valuables?" inquired Robber Thyme. – "Not so fast, buddy!" laughed Robber Rob. –

The PA distributed a form, four pages of small print per passenger. – "They have to declarrre theirrr valuables?" asked Thyme. – "No way, buddy. These are our terms and conditions. They all have to sign them, otherwise we can't rob them." – "We don't want any of them to sue us in court. Savvy?" – "Better safe than sorry, buddy! In a single lawsuit you can lose more money than you can earn in all your life as an honest robber."

Without any ado, all passengers signed the form. Except for one of them. He inquired something in Spanish. – *"¡Naturalmente, amigo!"* responded the PA. "Here you are, *señor*, the Spanish version of our terms and conditions."

Finally the PA could start collecting the valuables. "We accept all major credit cards," he announced to his esteemed patrons. "Personal checks? Of course we accept them as well. But, mind y'all: if your bank refuses to pay, it will cost you an extra thirty dollars penalty!"

Robber Thyme was still impressed by the four pages of terms and conditions. "But if someone rrrefuses to sign? What do you do then?" – "That's easy, buddy!" Rob and Jack grinned broadly. "We kill him! Dead men don't go to court! Savvy?"

Later Robber Thyme took the PA aside. "That killing … is that, eh, frrrequent?" – "No, sir, it's really rare. But every now and then we issue press releases highlighting such cases. You see, sir, we want the people to sign these forms straight away. Once they insist on getting in touch with their lawyers, a hold-up will take forever and a day!"

Thyme was satisfied: "Murrrderrr is not good forrr the business, that's my motto." - "That's indeed what we are taught in our trainings, sir," confirmed the PA. "Every accidental encounter is a chance to build up a recurring customer relationship! And dead customers never come back."

Thyme was even more impressed when he saw the cards that the PA handed to the patrons:

> *With Robber Jack, your satisfaction is guaranteed!*
> *If you are not 100 % satisfied,*
> *you will get your money back!*

"That can't be serrrious?" inquired Robber Thyme. – "Sure it is, sir," asserted the PA. – "And if somebody complains, he will be visited by a ferrrocious gunslingerrr?" – "No, sir, he or she will get his or her money back." – "He or she, forrr God's sake. I forrrgot the political corrrrrectness. But it is forrrged money, I suppose?" - "No, sir, no cash. Security first. Our policy, sir. We send a check." – "Fake ones then?" – "No, sir, real checks from the bank, not from our own print workshop. The customer will indeed get the money. Customer satisfaction is our highest aim!" – "So the Siblinghood of Rrrobberrrs is indeed losing money when somebody complains?" – "The Siblinghood? But sir!" the PA laughed, "You can't possibly think that we'd give customers a check drawn on our own account?"

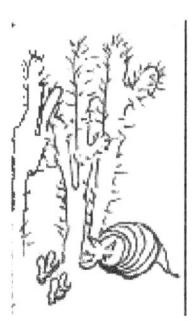

CHAPTER THE FOURTH

IN WHICH THIS ACCOUNT PROCEEDS TO THE GATES OF HELL, VIZ., A CALL CENTRE

On his free day, Robber Thyme went for a walk in the nearby park. While crossing the street, Thyme was almost hit by a cab, despite the zebra crossing. And who was sitting in the cab but the elderly gentleman with the black hat and the long coat? He waved apologetically. "He must be in a big hurrrrrry again to catch his flight," thought Robber Thyme.

Hermann Park had its centenary this very year. To celebrate this, they had demolished the rose garden and replaced it with a huge parking lot. Then they had constructed something that was supposed to function as an observation hill, only that it was not nearly high enough for that purpose, and thus rather resembled a mound, or a mole hill. Nevertheless, the people in charge of all this were very proud of their achievements. And the people who matter did not bother, for their golf course (which took up half the space of Hermann Park) had remained unmolested.

Thyme watched the water fowl swimming in the pond. Amongst the ducks and geese there was a swan who was pushing his way through the smaller species. "Make way!" Thyme heard the swan shout. "Make way, I'm the Texas-Sized Duck!"

"So this is how things worrrk herrre," mused Robber Thyme. "Forrrget about noble swans. Size matterrrs!" And indeed, for a duck, the swan was extraordinarily large.

Thyme walked back to the apartment that the Siblinghood of Robbers had arranged for him. It was in a tower within Houston's Museum District. A murder had been committed there – with a stiletto. How disgusting: it had been a really cheap pair of shoes! And the murderess was not even a licenced criminal. The Siblinghood of Robbers had sent their *consigliere*, Don Pacifico, to the owners of the building. Duly freightened, they agreed to let the apartment to the Siblinghood on very favourable terms.

Down in the hallway, Thyme studied an oversized billboard with announcements informing the residents when the elevators, the water, the gym or the swimming pool would be shut down for maintenance and repairs. A neighbour came along, and they started chatting. It did not take them long to find out that they were both Europeans. Dennis was not a robber, he was a businessman. An entrepreneur. Why he had come to Houston? "Pretty simple. Perfect city for me as a Slovak. Only major city in the world with no Hungarian restaurant!"

Thyme shook his head. "But Dennis is not a Slovak name?" he ventured. – "Of course not," his neighbour replied. "Back home, I'm Zdenko. But trust me, my business will be bankrupt before I find a customer who can pronounce that name!"

"What is yourrr business?" Robber Thyme wanted to know. – "Don't know yet," was the answer. "Working on the business plan." – "Keep me posted, neighbourrr!"

The next day at the Siblinghood of Robbers, Robber Thyme asked Robber Rob for one of his business cards. – "Here you go, buddy:"

> *Robber Rob – I live up to my name!*
> *Call now to make an appointment:*
> *1-800-ROB-ROBS*

"That reminds me, buddy," Rob said, "your cards ought to be ready today." And indeed they were:

> *Step back in time, get robbed by Thyme!*
> *Robber Thyme, our old-school European highwayman*
> *will rob you in style, like in your grandma's day!*

"Is this rrreally how you perrrceive me?" Robber Thyme was visibly irritated. "Hopelessly old-fashioned?" – "Oh, buddy, that's a super-duper business model! A first-class market niche, that's what our boss said!" – Fortunately for Thyme, Robber Rob did not repeat his remarks about sending Thyme to the Amish.

"And do the people rrreally call you forrr appointments?" inquired Robber Thyme. "Arrre they so keen to get rrrobbed?" – "Sure they are, buddy," explained Robber Rob. "That's the best for both sides. Win-win. Look, buddy, if I rob somebody who has no cash and no valuables on him, I get angry. I beat him up. Then he has to go to the hospital. Emergency room. Wait for six hours. Pay a hell of a lot of money. All his nice money going to the hospital, not to me. And he'll lose his wages for the day. Maybe lose his job because he didn't show up. Plus, it sure hurts a good couple of days where I hit him. So – why wouldn't any sensible person rather call in advance and make an appointment?!"

"And whom do people call?" asked Robber Thyme. "You have a perrrsonal assistant, Rrrob?" – "No, buddy. That's what we have our call center for. Super service. Come on, I'll show you."

Thyme had expected to be taken to a large room with a lot of people hanging on the phone. Instead, there was a giant mainframe computer with flickering monitors and control lights. "Here you see how many calls are being handled at any point in time, buddy," explained Rob with delight. "And our customer database is truly phenomenal!" – "And the people who take the calls, wherrre arrre they?" – "People? Ah, the people. Yes, no, well, eh, I'm not sure where they sit. Somewhere in Oklahoma, or even Montana. Out in the boondocks. They're all independent contractors. With home offices. That's cost-efficiency at its finest, buddy!" – Thyme scratched his head. – "Once, we outsourced our call center to India," continued Rob. "But it didn't work. Lots of customer complaints. That funny British accent over there!"

Later that day, Robber Thyme decided to give it a try. He called 1-800-ROB-ROBS.

"Welcome to Robber Rob's. Where can he rob you?"

"Good afterrrnoon. Robber Thyme calling."

Ouch. Why did he call using his real name? It did not matter. He was talking to a machine anyway.

"For English, press one. Por español, dos. For other languages, three. The numbers one, two, and three do not express a preference or a value judgement."

Political correctness, of course. The machine trilled on:

"For giving us feedback on a robbery, please press one.

To make an appointment for a street robbery, press two. For a burglary of your home or office, three.

If you want to order a burglary at your unfriendly neighbor's or your boss's, press four.

Do you need assistance in commiting an insurance fraud? Number five.

For job openings at the Siblinghood of Robbers, press six."

"Full serrrvice indeed!" Thyme was impressed. But it got even better:

"Are you with the police or in the legal system and looking for information about our cooperation program? Press seven. Back to the main menu, press zero."

Thyme chose number one – feedback on a robbery.

"Were you robbed in a building? Press one. In a vehicle? Press two. On foot? Three."

Thyme pressed the two.

"Were you robbed in your own car? Press one. In the car of your family or friend, press two. In a cab, three. On a bus, four.

If it was a city bus, press one. An interurban bus, press two.

Please enter the date of the robbery. Two digits each for month, day, and year.

Please enter the approximate time of the day in four-digit format, then one for a.m., or two for p.m."

Thyme was getting tired. But he went on.

"Please enter the number of the highway on which we robbed your interurban bus service."

Thyme tried to recall the number of the highway on which they had robbed the greyhound bus. He didn't remember. In his despair, he entered 99.

"On this highway, no member of our Siblinghood has performed a robbery on the date and at the time you entered. Please re-enter the number of the highway, or press the pound sign to correct date and time."

Thyme tried Route 66. That one should be a safe bet!

"On this highway, no member of our Siblinghood has performed a robbery on the date and at the time you entered. Please re-enter the number of the highway."

Thyme groaned. Would he have to try all the highways of the U.S. of A.? But this time, the announcement continued differently:

"If your entries were all correct, we have reason to suspect that you were robbed in an unlicensed manner, that is, by someone who had no proper credentials issued by our Siblinghood or by one of our accepted partner organizations. Please hold on to get connected to a service associate."

"Now comes the exciting parrrt", thought Robber Thyme.

"At the moment all our service associates are busy handling other calls from customers like you. Please hold on and listen to our awful music.

Unfortunately, all our service associates are still busy with their customer calls. Please stay on the line. You will be connected as soon as possible. In the meanwhile, here's our awful music again."

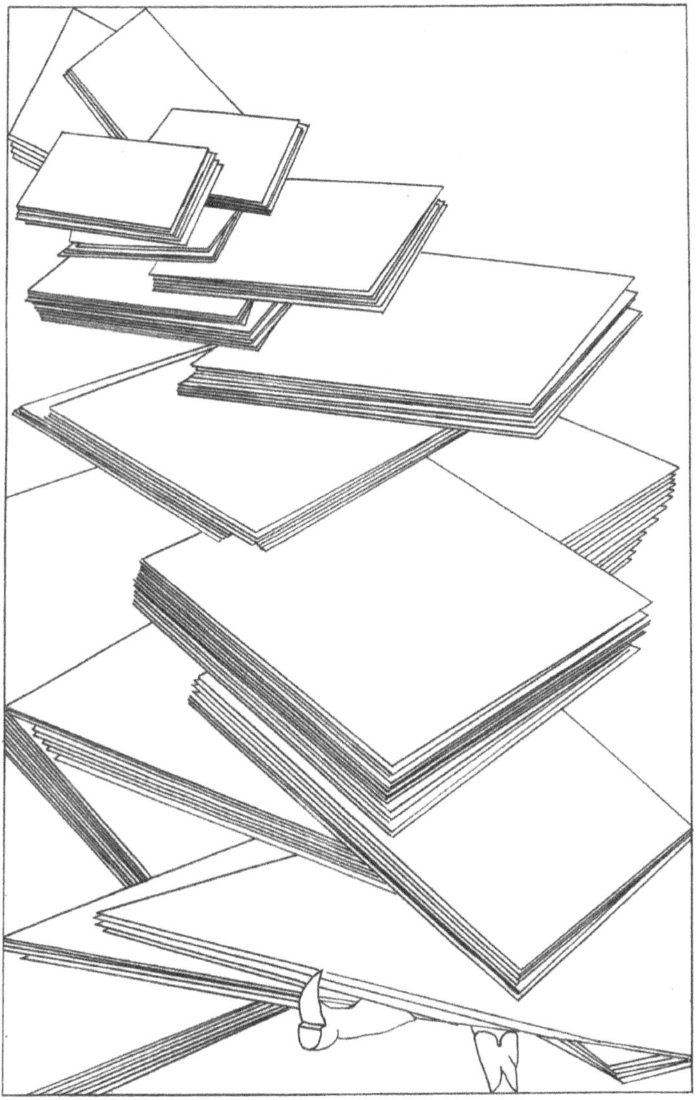

The seventh time that Robber Thyme heard this announcement, he threw his telephone against the wall. The telephone continued to play that awful music. But the wall now had a hole.

On that day, Robber Thyme was too frustrated to continue working. He left the office early. On his way home, he had an ice-cream, picked up some cough syrup from the pharmacy, and deposited money with the bank, all of that without having to get out of his car. Drive-thru businesses thrived everywhere.

Thyme chatted about this with his neighbour Dennis. "The people here just love their cars", explained Dennis. "They hate it every time they have to get out of them. Especially when they have to walk. In the open, without air conditioning!" – "So you can do everrrything frrrom yourrr carrr?" concluded Robber Thyme. – "Yes," was the answer. "Additional advantage: at some businesses, people cannot walk in with their gun. Very discomforting for a Texan. In a car you can have your gun, no problem."

Thyme had grown up in an environment where only licenced members of the Robbers' Guild were allowed to carry arms. And the police, of course. Tools of the trade, he thought. "And therrre's a drrrive-thrrrough forrr everrry business?" he inquired further. – "There's a niche left for me," asserted Dennis. "Trust me. I'll find it. I'm already working on the business plan."

At the office, Thyme told Robber Rob about his experience with the call centre service. – "Oh, that's very rare, buddy, don't you worry." Rob would not let anyone knock the Siblinghood's call centre. "And you should try the submenu where you report a burglary of your house. It's just awesome, buddy, I'm telling you!"

"Have we left your place in good condition so that we may come again? Excellent, press one. Good, press two. Satisfactory, three. Not fully satisfied, four. Unacceptable, five. This scale applies to the following questions, too.

Have we demonstrated taste and professional expertise in our selections from your paintings and jewelry?

Have we located all your most important valuables?"

"You'll neverrr everrr get an honest answerrr on that," Robber Thyme snorted. – "You bet, buddy, you bet! You wouldn't believe how gleeful these people can be! They are so happy if they can tell us that we didn't find the gold coins under the mattress, or we failed to take their genuine Andy Warhol because we thought it was only a poster!" – "You'll take carrre of that at yourrr next visit, I'm surrre." "We remedy that at our earliest convenience," stressed Robber Rob. "That's what we learn at our seminars, buddy: Every complaint is a gift!"

CHAPTER THE FIFTH

IN WHICH COMMUNICATION CHANNELS AND A CLASSROOM TRAINING ARE BEING TRUTHFULLY DESCRIBED

On his way out, Robber Thyme was stopped by Robber Jack. "Ahoy shipmate! Near Hermann Park is where you hang your hammock, right?" – "Beg parrrdon?" – "Your cabin! Your quarters, shipmate." – Thyme, still puzzled, answered in the affirmative. – "Then you wouldn't mind in the morning steering a course towards the bayou that runs alongside the park? Really important for the big brass on the quarterdeck, that job." – Thyme had to ask for an explanation of the term bayou. All right, he would walk over to that slow-running creek every other morning and pick up the dispatches that the Siblinghood's messenger would hand him there. – "Take this feather, so he'll recognise you," advised Robber Jack. "Savvy?"

The next morning found Robber Thyme walking on the shore of the bayou, feather in hand. A couple of joggers passed him, even a few bicyclists – a novelty in Houston in these years. But none reacted to the feather that Thyme was swinging more and more desperately.

"Stop! Will you stop!" came a cry from behind. Thyme stopped in his track, then turned around. There was his old acquaintance, the swan. "The Texas-Sized Duck!" as Thyme was immediately corrected. – "Here, take this, and bring it straight to the Robber Boss!" With these words, the duck (or swan) handed Thyme a message in a bottle.

Now Thyme understood why they had to meet on the bayou. – "A lot of trouble in times of drought," as Robber Jack would later explain. "You want to know where these messages come from? All right, I'll tell you: straight from the Chief of Police!" – "He is worrrking forrr ourrr Siblinghood?" Thyme was surprised. – "No, not the pirate hunter himself. But we are getting our drift bottles from right under his nose. From his very cabin! His rubber duck is in league with us. Savvy?"

A rubber duck in the police chief's own bathtub who would work for the Siblinghood of Robbers. Thyme agreed, these Americans were indeed advanced in their methods! "And why would she worrrk forrr us?" he inquired. – "Greed, shipmate, greed," was the answer. "She's corrupt. Has an expensive hobby. A pond in the garden. Fish. Japanese ones. Koi, they call them. Cost an arm and a leg! If a rubber duck had arms and legs, that is. So here we come in. Pay her out. Share of our booty."

"Arrren't messages in a bottle a bit slow?" Robber Thyme wondered. – "Safest channel of communication, shipmate. Ever heard of the NSA?" – Thyme had to concede the point. And the Robber Boss was delighted when

Thyme handed him the bottle. "For these messages she keeps shooting over to us, that rubber duck is worth her weight in gold!" the Boss declared. "Thank god, she's not an elephant."

"Action!" the Robber Boss cried a moment later. He summoned his secretary and his personal assistant. "Another first-class proposal from the rubber duck. An abducktion!"

Thyme was eager to be part of this adventure. Instead, he was cornered by two ladies. "We're HR," they introduced themselves. "Hennily and Rosalie. Just call us Henny and Rosy." Both wore membership badges of the Ebony Guild's Female Business Network. One of them had the stature of a sumo wrestler. The other was so slim that even Twiggy, if placed next to her, would look like a sumo wrestler.

Thyme would never find out which was which. Even the oldest members of the Siblinghood, a robber couple in their nineties known as Philemon and Baucis, could not tell them apart. And there was no need to know, they insisted. HR would always come as a pair. "That's efficiency," Henny and Rosy explained. "Either of us talks, the other is the witness."

Thyme ventured forth with the question why HR would want to meet him. He noticed the other robbers had all disappeared from sight. – "Just routine," HR reassured him. "You're a new kid on the block. You have to attend the newbie training."

So Robber Thyme spent the rest of the day in the Siblinghood's classroom. He didn't mind – lifelong learning had been his motto ever since. And his classmates were an interesting mixture. Hispanics who had traded their sombreros for ten-gallon hats. An English robber called John B who found it shocking that Starbucks would not serve decent tea. There were Italian Mafiosi in pinstripes and Borsalino fedoras. Russian Mafiosi pairing designer suits with white socks. A Japanese robber introduced herself as Michiko. Today she was in blue jeans and cowboy boots. She promised though to don her *kimono* and wear traditional wooden *geta* sandals, for more festive robberies.

Thyme was impressed by the ethnic diversity, and even more so by the docents. They all had a lively presentation style. The instructors at his Robbers' Guild back home all too often read from their manuscripts and had no rapport with their audience. Here, the Siblinghood's *Interfaith and Intercultural St Dismas, Robin Hood, El Maragato, Thief of Bagdad, Tajōmaru, Outlaws of the Marsh As Well As United Thugs and Dacoits (the Sequence Implying No Preference) Academy of Advanced Robbery* was certainly worth its tuition fees. (Participants were not permitted to pay with banknotes that could be traced to a bank robbery.)

The first docent gave an outline of the history of robbery in North America since Columbus. That great man could never have set sail without the active support of the Robbers' Guild of his time. The leading gaols of Spain had delegated their best and brightest inmates to his crew. A mere pickpocket would not have been allowed to join them, not even as a cabin boy.

On the *Mayflower,* too, there had been a criminal. The logbook had an entry that the captain's money pouch had been snatched. On a weekday, of course. A pilgrim cutpurse would never steal on a Sunday, except perhaps a horse to get to church on time.

All of a sudden the speaker had reached Jesse James, Bonnie and Clyde, then Al Capone. Thyme admired the presentation style, but he would have appreciated a bit more of German thoroughness. Not so the other robbers. They were already champing at the bit: no more history, give us practical hints!

That was exactly what the next speaker offered. As a starter, he recalled how in his early days he had almost been caught at a bank robbery. Not for doing the bank, mind y'all, but he had parked his escape car next to a fire hydrant!

School buses were another trap for an honest foreign robber unacquainted with American traffic rules. And the cigarettes! "Mind y'all, our Siblinghood has more members doing time in jail for having smoked in the wrong place than for honest crimes!"

"How about snuff?" Thyme desired to know. – "Can do," was the answer. "For now. Won't be long, though, that's my guess."

An entire section of the presentation was devoted to national holidays. "No holdups on Halloween. You get nothing but candies. And a stomach ache." – Independence Day was off limits as well, Thyme and his classmates learned. – "Robbing on the Fourth of July is unpatriotic, mind y'all. Except if you find a limey to rob." – Thanksgiving week had its rules as well: "Leave your victims enough money to buy a turkey. Don't ruin our holiday, boys, it's the biggest one we have."

"How about ethnic holidays then?" a participant wanted to know. – "An excellent question, this one. Thank you so much for asking it. For example, mind y'all, never pick the pocket of an orthodox Jew on Sabbath!" – "That would smack of anti-Semitism, wouldn't it?" – "An excellent question, that one. Thank you so much for … In fact, even worse. It would be pointless. They're not allowed to carry money on Sabbath.

Which brings me to the topic of discrimination," the speaker continued. "That's the most important of them all. Never give anyone the slightest reason to sue you for discrimination. If you're caught with that one, mind y'all, it will cost you more money in damages than you and your family can earn in three generations of robbery. And the Siblinghood won't come to the rescue, boys, not if it is about discrimination. We would face a class action pretty quick. Then the Siblinghood would be bankrupt, and good bye, honest robbery!

So listen up, boys. Never let a victim off the hook for anything. If there's a bunch of people, you rob all of them, rich and poor, young and old, black and white, fit and disabled. No pity, no exception, no discrimination. Leave any suckers out, boys, they'll find a lawyer, and you're out of business forever."

Languages were another important topic, the speaker stressed. All licenced robbers were obliged to have a flyer in dozens of languages, referring their esteemed patrons to the Siblinghood's translation hotline. "Your customers have the right to call them. If their own phone doesn't work, boys, you lend them yours." – "Why bother?" one of the participants demanded to know. Wouldn't everyone understand such basic phrases as 'Hands up!' or 'Your money or your life!'? – "An excellent question … What is this all about? That's right, boys, non-discrimination. Make sure to remember: Here in the U.S. of A., everyone has the right to be robbed in their native tongue."

A third speaker stressed the importance of always keeping proper tax records: "Y'all don't want to end up like Al Capone, right? So talk to Robber Karl-Wilhelm, our tax advisor, whenever you're in doubt. What? Does it takes a German to do these things right? You bet. Thank God we have enough German-stock people here in Texas! The filing system Karl-Wilhelm has taught us is mandatory, and I'll tell y'all now how it works."

Robber Q had the next turn. He hailed from Wales and had developed all kinds of technical gadgets for the Siblinghood. His latest achievement was an art detector app. It allowed a robber to scan every painting encountered in the course of duty, and to check it online against the demand of every registered fence in the art scene, even against the wish lists of those legendary art collectors in South America whose possessions never leave their vaults.

The last docent acquainted the robbers with the Siblinghood's customer loyalty programme. – "Thunderrr and Dorrria, what's that?" Thyme blurted out. "You werrre rrrobbed ten times, you get an extrrra hold-up on top?" – "Very good!" The speaker was undeterred. "That's almost how it works. The tenth time they are robbed, our frequent patrons get a voucher that can be used the next time they face a hold-up. When they surrender the voucher, they get away free, and the robber is compensated by the Siblinghood!"

Thyme was even more fascinated by the perks that the Siblinghood offered to their status customers. Silver customers received shopping vouchers, so they had a 15 % discount when they bought stolen goods (their own or somebody else's) from the fence. Gold customers got the additional privilege that, when robbed, they would have to surrender only 75 % of their money and valuables, the remaining quarter they were allowed to keep. – "And the platinum customers, for them we have a very special offer: return service! If we have robbed their most cherished possession, they just need to give us a call, and we'll bring it back and take something of equal market value instead."

Thyme was mesmerised. His Robbers' Guild back home had a lot to learn!

CHAPTER THE SIXTH

IN WHICH A BANK ROBBERY IS CONDUCTED IN JAPANESE STYLE

Robber Thyme was not an early bird, god forbid! But apparently one of his neighbours was. He was drumming the reveille at Thyme's door. - "Is the building on firrre?" grunted a disconcerted Thyme. – "Come on, it's my grand opening!" Neighbour Dennis was standing there, fully dressed. He had already mustered another neighbour. "That's Dr Matasano," he explained. "Works at the Texas Medical Center here." – Not very fond of making acquaintances at this ungodly hour, Thyme nevertheless dressed and followed his neighbours (by car, of course) to the site of the grand opening.

'Dennis' Drive-Thru Donuts' was written all over the place. Thyme expected himself and Dr Matasano to be the first customers. But who was there as first in the queue but the elderly gentleman with the grey goatee, the worn-out leather bag and the black ten-gallon hat! The Hispanic staff greeted him with a shy respect, and indeed he appreciated the place. "Great idea, such a drive-thru," he explained. "I've got no time to lose. The pilot of my flight to Washington won't wait!"

In order to be a good neighbour, Thyme ate a couple of donuts. But he sincerely wished Dennis had chosen a different line of business. The doctor, on the other hand, devoured the donuts in a way his dentist would have been pleased to see.

Later that morning, Robber Thyme stole a ten-gallon hat and a pair of cowboy boots. In his new apparel he drove to the Siblinghood of Robbers. He was in arrears with his paperwork. His travel expense claim for the trip from Germany had been rejected again. Thyme had attended online training on how to fill in the various forms for a U.S. working visa. The training fee was part of his expense claim. Which had been rejected, and Thyme had to find out why.

So he contacted the call centre. After ten minutes of awful music, a taped announcement:

"Welcome to the Siblinghood of Robbers' Centralised Travel Expense Claim Handling Center! Abandon all hope, ye who enter here. This call may be recorded for quality purposes."

Then, several steps with recorded multiple choice options, and at last a human voice to whom Thyme could explain. Or rather, he could voice his concern. He was informed that he had to submit his original receipt for said online training so that the Siblinghood of Robbers could get the German Value Added Tax reimbursed. – "But this is trrraining. Education is VAT-exempt." – "I understand your problem, sir, but you have to submit your original receipt so that the Siblinghood of Robbers can get the German VAT reimbursed." Thyme gave up and sent the receipt per e-mail.

A few hours later he had to contact the call centre again: "What? My trrravel expense claim was rrrejected again because I did not submit the orrriginal rrreceipt? Listen, this was an online trrraining. The trrraining website sent me the invoice perrr e-mail only. Therrre is no orrriginal." – "I understand your problem, sir, but you have to submit your original receipt so that the Siblinghood of Robbers can get the German VAT reimbursed. No, there is no need to use this kind of language. You just have to submit your original receipt so that the Siblinghood of Robbers can get the German VAT reimbursed."

Defeated, Robber Thyme printed the e-mail receipt, folded it, crumbled it, carefully placed a grease stain on it, and put it into an envelope addressed to the centralised handling centre. Back home he had never counted German bureaucracy among the things he might miss one day.

That afternoon, Thyme's mood was so gloomy that the Robber Boss started to worry about the morale of the troops. He was close to asking Robber Jack's PA for the departure time of the Greyhound bus to the edge of the next Amish community. Fortunately, Fauxbourdon le Brigand, a real Cajun robber from Louisiana, had a better idea: he would cheer up Robber Thyme by showing him a

state park with wild alligators (lethal accidents only every 200 years).

On their way they passed an area where travellers were warned not to give hitchhikers a ride due to the proximity of a prison. Thyme and Fauxbourdon were on the lookout for a chance to help out an escapee brother, but none emerged.

Then they were at Brazos Bend State Park. Less than an hour from Houston, Robber Thyme felt perfect tranquillity. And indeed there were a few alligators in the ponds! A long one with wide open jaws lay stretched out at the side of their hiking path! While this gator was staring at him, Thyme heard the other ones singing. It was a spiritual: *"Wade in the water, / Wade in the water, people, / Wade in the water, / Come on and feed hungry gators!"*

That evening, Robber Thyme wrote a long letter to the Robber Girl, Benedict the Short-Sighted Earthworm, and Jacob the Elephant who were taking care of Thyme's district while he was out. How exciting this New World was!

And how different in so many ways. For example, people in Houston were delighted when it rained, which was rare anyway. Back home in Thyme's Germany, people were not delighted when it rained. They would have to be delighted almost every day – and you can't expect that from a German.

The next morning (no donuts this time!), Robber Jack's PA caught Thyme right at the reception desk of the Siblinghood. "Sir! How are you? Glad to see you, sir. Important message from the Robber Boss. Today you're going to rob a bank with that Japanese Robber, Michiko."

Thyme's fatigue vanished in an instant. The PA shoved him into a meeting room where Michiko already waited. In *kimono*, *obi* and *geta* she was quite a sight. It must be stated that Thyme did not follow the PA's presentation with his usual attentiveness.

On their way out, a host of robbers came out of their cubicles to admire Michiko's attire. They were a bit disappointed that Thyme had not matched her *kimono* by wearing a *Lederhose*. "Thunderrr and Dorrria!" Thyme swore: "Beforrre I rrrun arrround like a Bavarrrian *Seppl*, I'd rrratherrr turrrn honest!"

A Wells Fargo branch was their designated target. Thyme imagined himself on horseback galloping after a stagecoach. No, they would take Michiko's pickup instead. She signalled to Thyme that he had to remove his cowboy boots. Once in the truck, Michiko insisted on ceremoniously offering her guest a cup of tea before starting the engine.

The bank was not far away, but they still lost their way twice. So many construction sites! Even more now because, like every two years, mayoral elections were near. Fortunately, Houston is inhabited by very friendly people.

(The few unfriendly ones must be from D-town, they are convinced.)

"Hi! How arrre you?" Thyme would ask, not trusting Michiko's English language skills. – "Fine!" was the inevitable response – "That's grrreat! Excuse me, we want to rrrob the Wells Farrrgo brrranch on Kirrrby Drrrive. How do we get therrre?" – "That's easy, hon! Make a U-turn, then right at the second traffic light, and right again!" – "Thanks a lot! Have a wonderrrful day!" – "You, too! And don't get caught, hon!"

Having arrived in front of the bank, Robber Thyme was glad to be reunited with his boots. But before he could even enter the building, a bored security guard stopped him, pointing at a sign at the door that prohibited firearms in the bank. – "But don't you have that second amendment?" Thyme mumbled in vain. – Meanwhile, Michiko gracefully skipped into the bank with an innocent smile on her face and a *samurai* sword in each hand.

Thyme waited outside and took a pinch of snuff, but got more and more morose. What was she doing in there for such a long time? "This is not the Gallerrria mall, is it?" cursed Robber Thyme. But maybe she had gotten herself into trouble? However unwillingly, Thyme left his two pistols in the car. Still with the three knives in his belt, he went after Michiko into the bank.

And what a scene unfolded before his incredulous eyes! There was Michiko in full motion, dressed to kill and brandishing her two *samurai* swords. Bank employees and customers alike watched with utmost fascination how the teller tossed one cheque form after the other into the air and how Michiko's whirlwinds of steel split them in two or even four pieces. And it seemed so effortless!

Thyme watched the elegant swordplay for a while. He cherished his good old knives, but they (and he) had their limits. Still he felt obliged to remind his fair partner in crime of the business they had to attend to. – "What?" – She did not understand. Thyme was tempted to grab her sleeve and draw her over to the teller's desk, but her whirling swords prevented him from committing such an unpardonable breach of *samurai* etiquette.

Instead he seized the teller, forced him to hand over the cheque forms to another colleague, and pulled him to his desk. The teller, with Thyme's knife at his throat, made superhuman efforts to change his position and regain an unobstructed view of Michiko's performance.

"Yourrr money orrr yourrr life!" Thyme had to repeat himself three times before the distracted clerk would react. Then the teller donned the standard smile that he had learned at the bank customer service training and grabbed from his desk – no, not a thick bundle of banknotes, but a flyer that Thyme had to read:

In order to give you a faster and more advanced professional service, our bank has centralized all business with our esteemed robber patrons and outsourced it to our specialized handling partner. Please call 1-800-ROB-BANK three banking days in advance to ensure your robbery will be a successful one!'

The message was repeated in a multitude of languages, including Japanese. Michiko could have used this translation. Thyme suspected she had started her sword performance only because the teller, when she asked him to deliver the money, did not understand her accent.

But with her performance Michiko was a success, Thyme had to admit that. The fascinated audience insisted on no fewer than three encores. Thereafter she had to sign a few autographs (in Japanese calligraphy, with ink and brush!) before they let her, however unwillingly, go.

Back at the Siblinghood of Robbers with empty hands, Thyme's face turned as red as his robber beard when he saw the PA. In the future he would pay closer attention to his briefings! But he was spared a report on their misadventure when Michiko showed the robbers what she had done with her *samurai* swords at the bank.

Aside, Thyme asked Robber Jack what would happen if someone really called 1-800-ROB-BANK. No doubt the police would dispatch a SWAT team to the bank if warned three banking days in advance? – "No, not if the call comes from a regular signalman in our crew, shipmate! As long as we stay within our assigned quota, we're fine. They maintain provisions for that in their balance sheet. Those organized banksters, they would never want to run afoul of us freebooters!"

CHAPTER THE SEVENTH

IN WHICH A CONCIERGE AND AN ARMADILLO MAKE THEIR APPEARANCE

A few days later, a heavy hand again banged on Thyme's door at an ungodly hour. Neighbour Dennis again, of course. He invited Thyme for dinner that evening. "Dr Matasano will be with us, too. Where? At my drive-thru of course!"

Donuts for dinner? Thyme's face must have expressed his opinion all too clearly. – "No donuts. I've moved on. Another guy is running the donut place for me now. See you tonight: at Dennis' Drive-Thru Diner! A very practical place: no trouble with valet parking, and no golf carts needed to take patrons to and from their cars!"

At the Siblinghood, Thyme was once again cornered by HR. They had just reprimanded John B the Englishman for discourteous behaviour towards a client: "You can't just interrupt a hold-up and let your customer wait!" – "But it was time for my tea interval!" he tried to argue. – "Customers first!" they insisted.

And now it was Thyme's turn. Henny (or was it Rosy?) vituperated him for having used profanity in his interactions with the call centre agent. She gave him the address of the website where all banned words were listed. "Same list that the Houston ISD uses, the Intransigent School District", added Rosy (or was it Henny?). "Every month, the list has to be read aloud in class so that the kiddos know which words they mustn't use."

"So the teacherrr rrreads out all the foul worrrds to the class?" – "Not the teacher anymore, hon!" Henny (or Rosy) trilled. "They changed that. Now it's the best in class who has the privilege of reading out loud the list of forbidden words. Makes some students work a lot harder, yes sir!"

Thyme promised to watch his language accordingly. Later he learned that the Robber Boss had assigned him to do an apartment together with Robber Raoúl, a colleague from south of the border. (Robber Thyme concluded that some of the other robbers must have been pulling his leg when they told him that a state law required all male Hispanics to use no name other than José.)

They departed immediately. Right after the siesta, that is. Thyme noted that Raoúl was by far the best-looking robber he had encountered so far. Except for his bow-legs, this true account is obliged to note. Raoúl was nevertheless proud of them: a token of his horsemanship, he claimed. So Thyme was slightly disappointed that they went to the garage and not to the stables.

First they had to get past the concierge who sat bored behind a polished desk. Face, body, cap, tie, uniform and the desk itself were all black, and Texas-sized, TX XL. (In fact, in Texas everything is Texas-sized, except for the Ferris wheels, which for some obscure reason are much smaller than the surrounding buildings.) Thyme wondered what story they should tell the concierge. That they were from the electricity company, or that they were the plumbers?

Robber Raoúl did not invest much fantasy: "The Masterson apartment. Yes, Mr. and Mrs. Masterson." – "Them with all that old stuff from Europe? They say it's freaking valuable, but for me it's just junk." – Thyme was distressed that Raoúl kept clattering his lock picks. Indeed the concierge inquired after the purpose of their visit. – „¿Beg pardon, *señor*? Yes, indeed, we are here to burglarize." – Thyme was flabbergasted. Not so the concierge: "Masterson. Fifth floor, third door on the left. Mind y'all, they're not at home today. But wait a second, I'll have to make a phone call first. You know our policy."

"Let's rrrun, he'll call the copperrrs!" hissed Robber Thyme. - „¡*Cojones, amigo!*" retorted the Mexican. – Astonished, Thyme watched how the concierge dialled a number and kept drumming on his polished desk while he had to listen to the music (which he even liked). At last he got connected. Thyme got nervous again when he heard the concierge spelling out the address. – "I'm telling you, he's calling the copperrrs! Move, beforrre it's too late!"

Raoúl grabbed Thyme's arm. And indeed, with a routine grin the concierge shoved them in. "Okey-dokey, folks, y'all's organization confirmed that y'all are genuine robbers. Sorry for the wait, but just last week we had a fake plumber here. Better safe than sorry, my friends!"

Robber Raoúl assured Thyme that the apartment had no alarm system. Why would he know that, Robber Thyme demanded to know. Had he asked the concierge, or bribed the cleaning-woman? Not at all, it turned out. The Siblinghood could obtain such vital information straight from the horse's mouth. Per city ordinance, Houston required all law-abiding citizens to obtain a permit if they wanted to operate an alarm system. The lists of all alarm permits issued were kept at city hall, and copied at regular intervals by a city clerk in league with the Siblinghood of Robbers (whose communication channel with the Police Chief we already know).

"And if we happen to burrrgle into an aparrrtment with an unlicensed alarrrm system, eh?" – "No reason to worry, *amigo*: if the alarm is unlicensed, the police will not come. ¡Or only to make the owner pay a fine!"

On their way out, the Texas-sized concierge remarked on their half-empty robber bags: "You agree their artsy crap isn't worth taking? The same happened when a couple of burglars came last year, my friends!" – "If no honest rrrobberrr will take theirrr stuff, one day theirrr heirrrs will have to donate it to a museum!" commented Robber

Thyme, while Robber Raoúl was clattering the jewellery they had found.

In the evening at Dennis' Drive-Thru Diner, Robber Thyme and Dr Matasano chose adjacent parking spots so that they could enjoy a conversation. With some acrobatics, Dennis occasionally got into one of their cars to chime in. The doctor was quite excited about the tax shelter that Dennis was explaining to him. For Dennis was already preparing his next outlet. Together with a Vietnamese buddy, he would open Dennis' Drive-Thru Dumplings!

Thyme was not surprised to see the elderly gentleman again, as usual on his way to the airport, but this time in a rental car. Thyme could not understand what the gentleman murmured before starting to eat. It sounded like an ancient and faraway language. Later, he heard the gentleman's eulogy for Dennis's businesses. "I'm telling you, sir, a true blessing, these drive-through establishments! Especially for people like myself! – As if there were people like myself, for that matter," he added gloomily before heading off for the airport. California this time, he said.

So apartments were an easy target, Thyme had learned. But surely the people who lived in villas had much richer booty to offer? On the other hand, many of them had gates and fences embellished with menacing signs. *We don't call 911,*' they promised, displaying pictures of guns and/or guard dogs that they would set loose on any intruder. Some of these signs were even more direct: *'Intruders will be shot dead. Support your local organ donor service!'*

"Yes, the Castle Doctrine," explained Robber Rob. "You'd better burglarize when folks are not at home, buddy. The guard dogs? They're no problem at all, buddy. Just bring the right kind of animal with you."

Working with animals was not a novelty for Thyme. In Germany, he had Benedict the Short-Sighted Earthworm as his assistant, and Jacob the Elephant had helped him with many robberies as well. Here in Houston, too, several robbers had animal companions. Robber Fauxbourdon the Cajun for example worked with a squirrel he had trained. Squirrel Louis would perform tricks to distract the patrons while Fauxbourdon snatched their wallets. Especially families will small children were grateful for this distraction. "Still cheaper for them than buying their kids the latest computer games all the time, *'ein?'*" explained Robber Fauxbourdon. "And of 'igher pedagogic value!"

So one evening Robber Thyme strolled through Hermann Park at night, equipped with a letter of recommendation issued by Benedict the Short-Sighted Earthworm back home. The swan, pardon me, the Texas-Sized Duck, had given Thyme directions to a spot where he could be sure to meet a trustworthy armadillo every night.

And indeed there she was. "Amanda," she introduced herself. "¡The sassiest armadillo in all of H-Town!" She explained her *modus operandi*. She would flirt with guard dogs if they were male. If female, she would lure those bitches to a rendezvous with some really hot dogs. In either case, the coast would soon be clear for Robber Thyme!

Why she would do that? Well, for her share of the booty she expected to get some emeralds and rubies. With these she would decorate her den. Yes, a gypsum owl would be appreciated as well. Funny that Thyme's home town would have the same animal mascot as Houston's Rice University. But for her robbery work she expected gemstones. "¡Tit for tat, baby!" she explained to an astonished Thyme. For many decades no-one had called him baby. Let alone an armadillo!

CHAPTER THE EIGHTH

ONE SIBLINGHOOD UNDER GOD

There they were. Henny and Rosy again. One from one side, and one from the other. No way to escape. Robber Thyme examined his conscience. For what might they reprimand him this time?

"Where do you worship?" asked Henny-or-Rosy. – "Worrrship?" echoed Robber Thyme. – "Yes, worship!" added Rosy-or-Henny. "Go to church! Or synagogue, mosque or temple. As you know, we have religious freedom here."

"Since you have rrreligious frrreedom, why do you carrre wherrre I go?" Robber Thyme argued. – "That's our policy!" said Henny-and-Rosy in unison. – "I'm serrrious," that was Thyme again. "How about frrreedom of rrreligion?"

Rosy-and-Henny threw a pitiful look at each other. Then they took a deep breath. "Of course we have religious freedom!" one of them asserted indignantly. – "You are free to believe whatever you want!" the other fell in. – "We don't discriminate whatever belief you have." – "Go to church on Sunday, go to the Synagogue on Sabbath, or to the mosque on Friday. We won't care." – "As long as you go somewhere. Hindu, Buddhist, Shinto temple, as you like." – "Robber Rob for example believes in the Flying Spaghetti Monster." – "Or take Robber Rick. He's Irish. Every Saturday evening you'll find him at the pub, writing limericks on religious topics." – "For us, one religion is as good as any other."

"And if someone happens to have no rrreligion at all? Can't a rrrobberrr be an atheist?" Robber Thyme demanded to know. – "No-one will demand that you believe in any god." – "Known or unknown." – "But we are a value-oriented organisation indeed." – "That's our policy." – "You have to have principles." – "You cannot just stay away from everything." – "You can't have a day off every week just for nothing." – "If you are an atheist, you have to attend an atheist assembly." – "To worship and celebrate that there is no god."

For now, Thyme got off the hook in return for a promise to make up his mind by next Sunday, or Saturday or Friday or whatever other day of the week it might be, the Siblinghood does not discriminate. Thyme's nostalgic thoughts wandered off to the monk in his hometown whom he had robbed from the cloister. The monk had decided to stay with the Robbers' Guild, and had established the Chapel of St Dismas the Good Robber for their services.

Here in Houston, Thyme talked with some of the other robbers in order to find an option suitable for him. Still he did not quite understand that atheist thing. "So if I don't carrre for football, baseball, basketball, orrr hockey, I would still have to go to the stadium on a match-frrree day and sit therrre forrr the durrration of a match?"

The irony was lost on his colleagues. Instead they explained that the policy of the Siblinghood did not prevent them from doing a little side job while attending the service. As long as they confessed their sins according to the rules of their respective religion.

For the Roman Catholics among them, these side jobs always led to heated debates. Said Irish Robber Rick, for example, worshipped at the Co-Cathedral of the Sacred Heart, but took the offerings from any Episcopal or Presbyterian church where the neighbourhood appeared to be affluent enough. "Better let the others bleed than my own people!" was Rick's motto.

Hispanic robber and money forger Fabio had been educated in a Jesuit school. He declared that heresy. *"¡Principiis obsta,"* he thundered, "resist the beginnings! ¡If you rob the offerings of one of those protestant conventicles, it's the first step towards recognising them … as if they were, god forbid, a real church! If they insist on being robbed, they are most welcome to come to Our Lady of Walsingham. That's Anglican liturgy, but with the Pope's blessing."

"Arrre therrre that many churrrches in Houston?" inquired Robber Thyme while taking a bit of worldly comfort in the form of snuff. – "More than enough, buddy!" explained Robber Rob. "Try a different one every Sunday, and you'll be busy for years to come!" – Robber Jack suggested they start from the top: "There is one church, shipmate, where Gott himself is preaching every Sunday! The Reverend Michael Gott of the Unity congregation. Not to be confused with Joel Gott, the Californian winemaker. Savvy?"

Apropos wine: Robber Fabio accused some of those suspicious Protestants of attending their so-called churches for the wrong reason, namely for getting a sip of wine before 12 noon on a Sunday – which in a bar, or even a grocery store, would be against Texas law.

Being German, Robber Thyme asked for a systematic overview of Sunday services. For that purpose, there was no better source than Robber Ezekiel. He had an encyclopaedic knowledge of all churches found in the Greater Houston Area.

"Adventists of the Seventh Day," he started in alphabetic order. "Anabaptist-Mennonite. Armenian Orthodox. Mind you there are two of them, brother. Baptists, among which: First Baptist Church, with the motto: 'If your life stinks, we have a pew for you.' Second Baptist Church. Third Baptist Church, not available here – congregation dissolved. Fourth Baptist Church, they just split, so you can go to the Fourth-and-a-half Baptist Church, brother. Fifth Baptist Church. General Six-Principle Baptists. Seventh Day Baptists. Praise the Lord."

Robber Thyme wondered how many hours (or days?) it would take Robber Ezekiel to reach Z like Zion. "In Amerrrica, do you rrread the gospel as 'Forrr wherrre two or thrrree are gatherrred togetherrr in my name, let them build thrrree or fourrr churrrches?!'"

Robber Rick commented that, in his humble opinion, most Houstonians were following only one religion: food. That is, dining out. – Ezekiel pressed on with his list: "Christian Rosicrucians, if you call them a church, brother. Christian Science. In Houston, there are 1st, 4th, 7th, 8th and 9th. When one of them closes, the remaining ones ain't getting no new numbers. Praise the Lord. Cowboy Churches: Lone Star of Bethlehem, Ox of Bethlehem (a Longhorn, of course)."

Robber Thyme was getting impatient. He was ready to take just any church. – "Don't talk like that, brother! It offends the Lord. Deciding which church you go to is a very serious matter. If you make the wrong choice, brother, you'll regret it for all eternity!" – "This is Texas, O.K., buddy?" Robber Rob had rejoined them. "Let's take the biggest church there is." – "God is great," agreed Robber Ezekiel.

Next Sunday found Robber Thyme, united with (in alphabetical order) Robbers Ezekiel, Rick and Rob, on their way to church, all in Sunday suits, bible in hand and guns neatly polished. The One and Only Texas-Sized Mega-Megachurch was their destination. It claimed to be larger than even Lakewood Church! Robber Jack's PA would not join them there. He was convinced that attending service at a more exclusive congregation would give a better push to his career.

Thyme was impressed by the streaming crowds. Although it was just a regular Sunday (Robber Rick had called it the 67th of Ordinary Time), the mega-megachurch had hired plenty of off-duty police officers for parking control. There were more officers buzzing around in the various parking lots here than attendees at an average congregation in a German city!

"Welcome! Jesus loves you!" every single soul was assured by the ushers. – "It is always fruitful to attend a service," promised Robber Ezekiel. – The building did not look very church-like: it could not hide the fact that it had served as an indoor stadium for many years. But Thyme was ready to admit that the stable at Bethlehem had not been a regular church either.

The service of course began with "How are you?" – "Fine!" Then hymns were sung, with more verses and melody variants (all simultaneous) than Thyme had ever heard before. There was no liturgy, but that did not disturb the excited congregation. They followed the sermon enthusiastically, throwing in "Hallelujah!" and "Praise the Lord!" at regular intervals. Then prayers were said, and several members of the congregation recounted how Jesus had intervened in their lives.

"Heads up!" signalled Robber Ezekiel with the help of his elbows. "Now comes the offering!" – "Brothers and sisters, give most generously!" shouted the preacher. – "Hallelujah!" responded the congregation. – "Again I tell you," declared Robber Ezekiel to the crowd, "It is easier for a camel to go through the eye of a needle than for someone who is rich to enter the kingdom of God." – "Praise the Lord!" the other Robbers fell in. – "Give back to God what is God's!" continued the preacher. – "You cannot serve both God and money!" responded Robber Ezekiel. – "Hallelujah!"

The preacher again: "Mind y'all: God does not want to see George Washington!" - Robber Thyme did not understand the theology behind that. But Robber Ezekiel did. "Nor Abraham Lincoln," he fell in, raising from his pew. "Nor Alexander Hamilton." – "He will consider Andrew Jackson if He's given no other choice," asserted the preacher. "But He does prefer Ulysses Grant." – "Even more so, Benjamin Franklin. Best of all if he doesn't come alone."

Supported by the congregation with thundering "Hallelujahs", the robbers accompanied the ushers through the hallways and collected the offering. "God accepts personal checks," they proclaimed to the believers. When a few misers hesitated, the robbers would cut their purses and throw them into the collection basket under general applause. What, there was someone who would offer resistance? "I have a telling argument for you, brother," trilled Robber Ezekiel, "from Saint Paul's letter to the bladesmiths of Toledo in Spain! And," he added with a significant move towards his belt, "I even have their answer here, very much to the point!"

The ushers welcomed the help, since indeed the collection baskets had become very heavy. But suddenly they realised that the four robbers, guns and daggers in hand, were making it for the exit. "Brother!" explained Robber Ezekiel to the disconcerted preacher. "You cannot serve both God and money!"

Houston's finest helped the robbers merge right into traffic. On their way back to the Siblinghood, they counted their booty. Thyme was more than impressed. Even at Cologne Cathedral, seat of the richest bishopric in Christendom, it would take many a Sunday to raise such an amount!

Robber Ezekiel reminded them of their duty to tithe. So they made a detour to a church called Centurion of Capernaum, known to be frequented by law-enforcement officers and their families. Throwing ten percent of their booty into the collection box earned them a standing ovation from the congregation.

The other robbers at the Siblinghood praised their success. Most fascinated was Chi Ting, a robber girl recently arrived from China. Robbing places of worship was a completely new area of business for her. The Chinese are far too smart to use real money for offering at their temples. They use special ghost money instead!

CHAPTER THE NINTH

A VILLA JOB, AND OTHER PASTIMES

Robber Thyme wondered whether his neighbour, too, would discover how lucrative religion could be. Deacon Dennis' Drive-Thru Divine Service, didn't that sound great?

Together with Dr Matasano, Thyme drove over to Dennis's new dumpling place for dinner. Not an easy task to eat dumplings while sitting behind the steering wheel, especially with chopsticks! They spotted how the ubiquitous elderly gentleman dropped one on his trousers. How unpleasant for somebody so far away from home and with no time to lose! But: "No problem, *Su Eternidad*," said the Hispanic waiter. (Thyme was surprised. Had he misheard the title?) "¡Dennis's Drive-Thru Dry-Cleaning is just around the corner!" the waiter continued. "Special service, *Su Eternidad*: they clean your trousers while you keep driving around the block!" (So Thyme had not misheard. *Excelencia* he would have understood. But why *Eternidad*?) – The doctor wondered whether the cleaners would lend the gentleman a beach towel in the meanwhile. – "¡Certainly they'll do that, for a small service charge, doctor-sir!"

The next day Robber Thyme would do one of those posh villas in West University. A nearby one sported a sign: *'We don't dial 911, and we don't call the ambulance – but leave your heirs' address here, we can recommend a first-class undertaker!'* Compared to that, the target villa's sign was almost conciliatory: *'We give warning shots only if prepaid. Insert cash here. Otherwise we shoot on sight.'*

Thyme's first collaboration with Amanda the Armadillo! She assured him that all the human inhabitants had already left. The private security patrol had just passed, so they would have at least an hour before their next round. Amanda went ahead to seduce the guard dog. Soon she beckoned that Thyme could follow. The Great Dane just sat and smiled.

True to his principles, Robber Thyme checked the escape routes first. Besides the usual veranda doors, even the guest toilet had a second door to the outside. No need for a lover, or an honest robber, to hide in the closet nowadays!

Then he checked the rooms. The TV set had its own room. It had such a large screen that Thyme thought he had confused the address and burgled into a movie theatre, not a private home. The refrigerator could have served a medium-sized cinema as well. It was larger than the walk-in closet at Thyme's apartment.

But where were the valuables? While the enamoured guard dog was massaging the armadillo's unarmoured belly, Thyme searched the house. Back and forth, and forth and back, but to no avail. In desperation, he turned his eyes towards heaven. Lo and behold, there was his booty: they had decorated the ceiling of their dining room with leaf gold!

Cursing like a sailor, Thyme procured a ladder and tools to scratch the leaf gold off the ceiling. This was the hardest work he had ever done! "Folks in the 19th centurrry came to Amerrrica thinking that the strrreets werrre paved with gold. Little did they know!"

After almost an hour, Amanda urged him: "¡Time's up, baby!" – Thyme still winced at this form of address.

But he was elated to see how much delight Amanda took in her share of the booty. "¡The leaf gold will look so beautiful on my ceiling! ¡My den will be the fanciest in all of Texas!"

So this had been a profitable job. Although in general Thyme preferred hold-ups over burglaries. What he most enjoyed in his trade was the contact with people.

People in abundance he soon had at the Houston Livestock Show and Rodeo, a three-week event held every Spring. Thyme enjoyed the rodeo competitions, the cattle show, and the whole fun fair atmosphere. The classical disciplines like calf roping, bull riding and barrel racing were held every day. Robber Raoúl, the Siblinghood's chief expert in all matters equestrian, explained the rodeo rules to Robber Thyme, never leaving out an opportunity to point out how much the cowboys of old had learned from the originals, the Mexican *vaqueros*. Thyme was a bit disappointed that Raoúl was not on horseback.

One day was designated as Robbers' Day. On that day, the Siblinghood would organise its own contests, such as handbag lassoing, kidnap roping, and guard dog deceiving. Robbers and animals from all over the U.S. and Canada would come to compete for cash prizes and medals. Raoúl did not compete. Tennis elbow, he claimed.

Ancient craftsmanship was honoured as well: horse-traders and cattle rebranders demonstrated their skills. Then there was the barbecue competition. This was by far the most dangerous event of the whole rodeo. True, riding wild horses and vicious bulls led to the occasional broken limb, but far more bruises, black eyes and other injuries were meted out in disputes over time-honoured family recipes.

The Siblinghood had its own provost marshal. He handled recalcitrant robbers who did not follow the dress code, or used foul language towards customers. But on BBQ day he and his troops would not even pretend to maintain law and order. When it came to carcass cooking, they were passionate, as behoves a Texan.

But there was still Robber Lennart, the Siblinghood's safety officer. He used all his non-Norwegian eloquence (some people have to emigrate for a reason!) to keep the squabblers apart. But when one of the quarrellers compared the scent of his opponent's barbecue sauce to that of *lutefisk*, and did not exactly mean that as a compliment, Lennart's dispassionateness was over in an instant, and he took as great a part in the general merriment as any other member of the Siblinghood.

The next day at the Siblinghood, Robber Thyme, bruised and battered but undefeated in the cause of German *Currywurst*, inquired about some entertainment that was usually less likely to result in the loss of life and limb: how about classical music in Houston? He was referred to Robber Amadeo who was the authorised expert on the concert scene.

He had a degree from Houston's renowned Rice University. The institution had originally been called Noodle University after Nehemiah Williamson Noodle, its founder, but had recently been renamed in order to attract more Asian students.

Robber Amadeo's hold-up days were over, but he fulfilled a most important role. Wearing glasses and a beret (which he never removed, not even in church) but not a full beard (although the policy of the Siblinghood did allow that for semi-retirees), he attended each and every concert that took place anywhere in Houston. To musicians who distinguished themselves, he handed out seals *"By appointment to the Siblinghood of Robbers"* which they could attach to their instruments so that they would not be stolen.

A less coveted seal he attached in a clandestine manner: musicians received one when Robber Amadeo opined that, in the interest of a discriminating public, their instruments should be stolen at the first opportunity!

Robber Thyme was very pleased with the music scene in Houston. Especially chamber and baroque music were performed at an extraordinarily high level. In addition to the Grand Opera, there was a chamber opera, an intimate place where Thyme felt as if he was attending a private performance at a nobleman's palace. Another advantage was that every programme included a name list of donors. It was always useful for the robbers to be directed to the affluent people in town!

He was surprised though by the rather unfanciful attire that seemed to prevail in the concert scene. "It is what it is," explained Robber Amadeo. "If you want to see people in fancy dresses, you need to go on a weekend, preferably after church or before synagogue, to an upscale grocery store where the ladies buy their politically correct, gluten-free, lactose-free crunchy granola from happy grains, all organic and wholesome!"

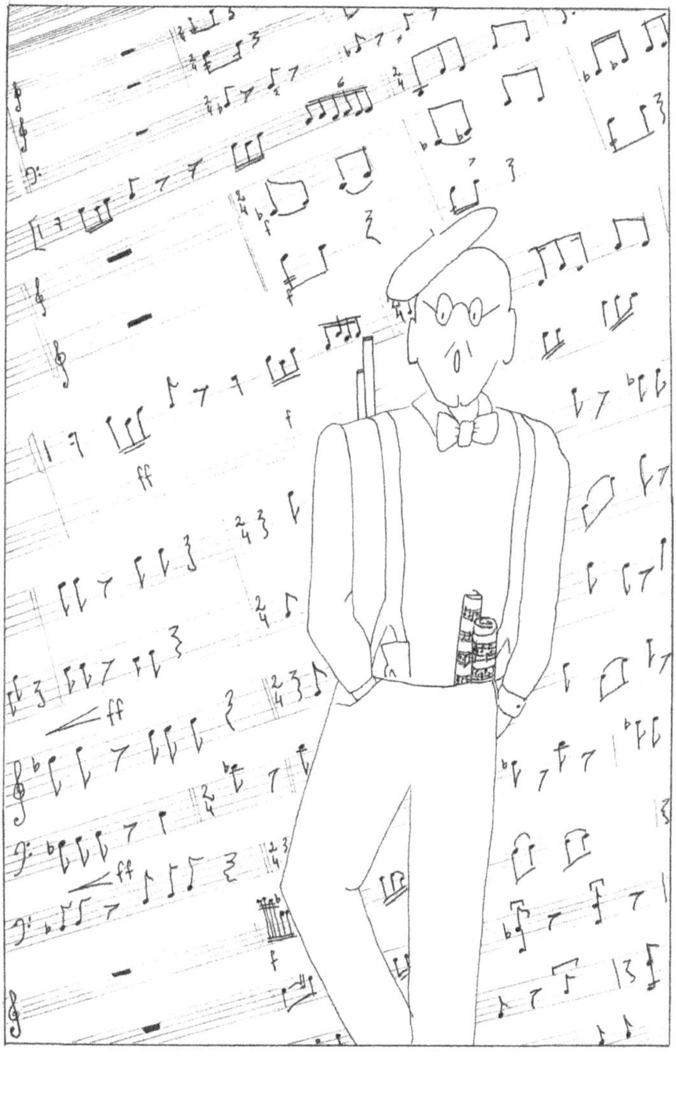

CHAPTER THE TENTH

IN WHICH THE HEAT BECOMES INTOLERABLE SO THAT ABDUCKTION BECOMES A MUCH MORE AGREEABLE OCCUPATION THAN STREET ROBBERY

On a day that looked no sunnier than any other, the sudden heat and humidity hit Robber Thyme like a sledgehammer. By the time he had reached his car in the parking garage, he was bathed in sweat. Thyme began to understand why walking or even outdoor dining was not really popular in Houston.

At the Siblinghood, Henny-and-Rosy laughed at him: "Now you know why we never schedule a delegation to Houston to start in the summer!" said one of them. And: "Mind you: it has to get worse before it gets better!" comforted him the other. Thyme could not imagine worse heat than today. But he was satisfied to note that even the local robbers were suffering.

Rosy-and-Henny rushed back to their cubicles to send a reminder to all robbers regarding the dress code of the Siblinghood. *Think of our reputation! Females, no sleeveless or tank tops. Males, no sandals, let alone flip-flops, except for beach jobs in Galveston.*

Galveston Island in the Gulf of Mexico! What an irresistible place for a Houston robber during the hot season! They bombarded HR with reasons why they should be assigned to jobs on the beaches instead of downtown Houston. But both HR and the Robber Boss remained firm. Like every summer, the robbers would have to take turns.

Street robbery was totally out during the hot months. The parks were safe, only there were no people in them to benefit. The robbers offered happy hours to lure people out of their air-conditioned houses and offices. They discussed business models that would not expose them to the merciless heat. And even an old-fashioned craftsman like Robber Thyme had to admit that Internet fraud in times like these had its advantages.

His regular walks to the bayou to collect the dispatches from the swan (pardon, the Texas-Sized Duck) became downright painful. He understood that Houston as a city had not really been able to grow properly before the invention of air conditioning.

But one of these bottles contained a message that electrified Thyme and his colleagues at the Siblinghood. The business proposed was a kidnapping or, as the duck liked to call it, an abducktion. O.K., the act itself would involve some outdoor activity, but then you could stay indoors composing letters, and would not have to go out again until the handover.

Two old ladies were the targets. Thyme recognised their names from the donor lists in the concert programmes. In good standing with their families, the duck's message asserted. One would not want to kidnap people whose families were actually glad to get rid of them – they would send no ransom, at best a lukewarm thank-you note.

Thyme's proposal to kidnap them on the way back from a concert was accepted by his colleagues. He added: "Nearrr a concerrrt hall we can carrrrrry ourrr guns in violin cases without rrraising suspicion." Thyme the traditionalist liked his idea, but his colleagues derided it. "What a greenhorn you still are. This is Texas, buddy! Guns carried openly won't raise anyone's suspicion here!"

In anticipation of both the music and the kidnapping, Thyme entered the concert hall at the Humbug Center for the Performing Arts. Of course Robber Amadeo was there in his beret. Thyme recognised a few more people whom he had seen at other concerts before. Some were even greeted by the musicians as they stepped onto the podium. A poor sod who kept coughing all the time was not scolded and sent home, but provided with cough drops. This was Houston at its best! And over there sat the two ladies he had come to abduct. He recognised them easily from the photos in the society columns.

On the way out after the last encore, everything developed as planned. Robber Michiko had been instructed not to bring her *samurai* swords and not to wear *geta* this time. In her high heels she looked like the walking stiletto murderess. So it was not difficult for her to distract the ladies' companions while Robber Jack and Robber Thyme, in the best tradition of Southern chivalry, took care of the two ladies. They allowed themselves however to deviate slightly from the chivalry protocol, at the end of which deviation the two ladies sat in two comfortable but not too spacious cells in a storage building ($ 1 buys first month's rent!).

The old lady abducted by Robber Jack kept admirably calm, even trying to start an exchange of opinions on the performance of the string quartet this evening. (In vain, for when it came to music, Robber Jack had never ventured beyond 'What shall we do with the drunken sailor?')

Robber Thyme was less lucky. His old lady complained all the way to the hideout: "What are you thinking? You cannot simply kidnap me like this! If you want to abduct me, I have to be joined by my personal shopper!"

Indeed it was the Siblinghood's policy to keep their clientele happy at all times, but never more so than during an abduction. It is irritating enough when people talk badly about you behind your back, but much worse having to listen to their harangues while you are guarding them! O.K., you could gag them, but remember that you have to return them to their paying families in good shape.

Thus Robber Jack and Robber Thyme willingly stole two TVs and set them so that the old ladies would not miss their favourite shows. And they organised food only from those restaurants that even the harsher of the two would approve of.

After three days, the robbers notified the families. Not earlier, for they wanted them to be duly worried. The first family responded by begging for instructions as to where and how they should provide the ransom. The other, by sending a detailed list of dietary instructions. The robbers did their best to comply: a lawsuit for damages is always dangerous, but it can be an honest robber's ruin if the costs of medical treatment are included!

In their second message, the robbers stated the ransom they demanded. The first family explained they needed more time to raise the amount. The other tried to negotiate, which would take time as well. So there was more time for the old ladies to show the robbers photos of their lovely grandchildren.

"Excuse me, young man, which day of the week is it today?" asked the kind old lady one day when Robber Thyme was on guard duty. – "Wednesday," was his answer. – "Would you then please give word to my congregation that I am so sorry to miss choir practice tonight, for I have been abducted!" – "Cerrrtainly, Ma'am! I'm surrre the choirrr dirrrectorrr will underrrstand. The choirrr memberrrs might even help yourrr family to rrraise the rrransom!" – "An excellent idea, young man! You will certainly make your way in your profession."

The harsh old lady, too, had her obligations. "For more than sixty years, I have had my game of bridge every Thursday. You cannot possibly think of making me miss that, abduction or not." – Robber Thyme could not agree to give her leave. Instead he promised to procure bridge partners for her here at the hideout. – "We have a number of professional gamblers in our Siblinghood, sir" asserted Robber Jack's PA whom Thyme had asked for help. "Black Jack or Texas hold 'em, anytime! But bridge?"

Thyme thought Robber Amadeo would be old-fashioned enough to be able to step in. And indeed: "Play Bridge? Sure, I know four people who can play Bridge. Look here, next week Thursday at Rice University: a string quartet playing Bridge! Frank Bridge, the teacher of Benjamin Britten." – "Benjamin who?" – "Benjamin Britten! The first English composer since Henry Purcell, with the possible exception of Edward Elgar. (Händel being counted as German, of course.)"

With the help of Robber Michiko, Robber Thyme solved the problem by blitz kidnapping two more old ladies from a nearby retirement home. Michiko was in her kimono again, so it was easy to convince the two ladies that they were all going to a masked ball (with Thyme in the costume of a robber, of course) and they had to be blindfolded. At the exit, the attendant on duty stopped the little procession, but only to have Thyme sign a liability release form.

The bridge evening had been a success. Meanwhile the first family had raised the money to pay the ransom. The family of Naomi the kind old lady. Robber Jack and Robber Thyme discussed the tempting option of releasing the harsh old lady instead. "We could say it was an honest mistake," chuckled Jack. – "A clerrrical errrrrrorrr." Roared Thyme. – Robber Jack's PA said this reminded him of a case study in business ethics he had done at Texas Christian University. And, by the way, didn't the Siblinghood, like every other respectable organisation, have a whistleblower programme? - "We were just kidding, cabin boy," assured Robber Jack melancholically.

The handover was to take place on a Saturday morning at the Farmers' Market on Richmond Street. Thyme knew that nothing was more suspicious than a secret meeting at midnight in a lonely area. But now in the hot season, why would it have to be outdoors?

"That's exactly why, sir," explained Robber Jack's PA. People will be so eager to get back into their air-conditioned car, they will look neither left or right." Indeed nothing was left to chance. Several robbers, trying to look granola-ish, surveyed the scene. And a message had arrived via the Texas-size duck confirming that Houston's finest did not plan any foul play.

Following the PA's plan, Thyme had filled an environmentally correct shopping bag with a variety of produce that would make a rabbit breeder green with envy. Naomi's family had been instructed to carry the ransom in a similar bag with a little bit of lettuce on top. Robbers Rob and Ezekiel had shadowed them from their home to make sure they would not get robbed on the way.

Robber Michiko distracted the bystanders with a question about the best route to Galveston. On a hot Saturday morning like this one, the Interstate would be hopelessly clogged. Everyone had a personal preference on how to bypass the traffic jam. The lively discussion gave Robber Jack all the time in the world to verify the contents of the bag that the family had brought. While apparently caring for nothing but green salad, he checked the greenbacks in the bag.

Finally Jack gave the all clear. Naomi embraced Thyme, Jack and Michiko, shared a few last pictures of her grandchildren, and reminded them always to wear a hat, lest they suffer a sunstroke. Then she departed with her family.

"Not so fast!" intervened the PA. "Ma'am, you need to fill out the questionnaire first. It's a very important document: our customer satisfaction survey!" – "You will do that for me, young man, won't you? Just write I was most satisfied with everything! I felt very much at home with you folks!"

The family was not exactly pleased when they heard this. But the robbers took no offence. Indeed they hoped that Naomi's family would manage a speedy recovery from the financial loss. This old lady was such a dearie, they would love to kidnap her again!

CHAPTER THE ELEVENTH

IN WHICH THE ABDUCKTION IS BEING CONTINUED, UNTIL A TURNING POINT IS REACHED

The other old lady was a much harder nut to crack. Her family had the liquidity, but they had left the communication with the robbers to their family lawyer. So the Siblinghood, too, had to involve their legal department, that is, Don Pacifico their *consigliere*. Punctilious clauses, each with a plethora of sub-clauses, were discussed back and forth. The family insisted on retaining part of the ransom for a certain period of time. This was to cover possible damages in case the old lady had latent defects that even in a sophisticated acceptance procedure (supervised by both the family doctor and a surgeon retained by the Siblinghood) could not be discovered at the time of return.

In return, Don Pacifico demanded a lien on the family's assets to protect the robbers in case the ransom turned out to have been paid in banknotes that were counterfeit, that originated from another robbery, or that were in consecutive numbers.

Draft clauses were sent by each party to the other, only to end up in a bloodbath of red ink. References to famous precedence cases in the legal history of Texas (under six flags!) were proposed and rejected. Robber Thyme thought that, even now in the hot and humid season, a simple street robbery might be preferable.

While there was no significant progress in this matter, the atmosphere in the Siblinghood's office building grew tenser and tenser. This happened every year. The long months of heat and humidity made the robbers quarrelsome.

This year food trucks were the hot topic. The building had no canteen. Therefore every day one of the Hispanic robbers had to go out, hijack one of Houston's many food trucks, and direct it to the building on Richmond Street where the hungry robbers were already waiting.

The Hispanic robbers did not mind that this task always fell to one of them. It was a time-honoured custom that all menial jobs were performed by Hispanics. Nobody could imagine it otherwise. Not even the Labor Council for Latin American Advancement (Latin Farmers Not Welcome!) would dream of changing that.

No, it was the non-Hispanic robbers who protested against this arrangement. Airport Eddy and Phil the Felon (whom Thyme had seen in action on the memorable day of his arrival to Houston) were the ringleaders. They were fed up with being fed tacos and tamales every single day.

The Robber Boss understood that the situation called for his leadership. He ordered Henny and Rosy to work out a plan which would ensure that all ethnic groups among the robbers (and among the food truck entrepreneurs!) were duly represented in the monthly schedule. So one crisis had been averted. Only John B the Englishman kept complaining that the Siblinghood refused to hire a tea lady.

At the storage building, the harsh old lady became more demanding by the day. Robber Jack's PA announced he would rather return to an honest life than to run all the errands she expected of him. And her food requirements were a severe strain on the robbers' budget, especially since she urged them to adhere to one set of dietary requirements while her family (supported by threatening missives from the lawyer) insisted on another.

"Shipmates: I can't stand this any longer!" cursed Robber Jack. "Let her walk the plank, and we sail on!" – "You amateurs!" scolded the harsh old lady. "The kind of letters that you keep dictating to me: no wonder my family wouldn't pay!" – "Rrreally?" Robber Thyme was desperate enough to give her a try at it. – And indeed the harsh old lady (whose name was Mildred, by the way) composed a letter that caused her family to double their ransom offer. Still a pittance, even after the increase, but more it was than the combined efforts of Robber Jack and Robber Thyme, supported by *Emily Post's Etiquette and Style*

Guide for the Successful Kidnapper, had yielded in several weeks.

Her next letter was even more effective. "My kidnappers are most cruel!" she wrote. "If you don't pay what they demand, they'll switch off the A/C in my dungeon!" – Thyme and Jack were so impressed that they allowed Mildred to offer her services on a commission basis to other robbers who had a demand for beautifully wordsmithed ransom letters.

At her suggestion, Dr Matasano generously provided them with blood from his practice so that they could apply ghastly-looking stains to each letter. In the blood group of the kidnapped, in case the family would care to have it analysed.

"They say in my church that I'm a scary fundraiser," explained Mildred. "Writing letters is not even my main strength. Wait till you see me visiting a home or, even better, an office!"

It was against custom and usance to allow a kidnapping victim to roam free. But at the Siblinghood of Robbers so many members were in arrears with their membership dues that the Robber Boss agreed to make an exception. Mildred was successful beyond imagination. Robbers, pimps and cutthroats queued in line to pay their overdues. Several of them even volunteered to increase their regular membership contribution. Mildred had made them an offer that they could not refuse.

The robbers begged the Robber Boss to agree that Mildred would use her impressive talents on the outsiders instead of on members. As soon as all overdues were paid, he agreed.

There was no apprenticeship here like back home in Thyme's Robber Guild, no vocational training school and no journeyman's piece. To become a member of the Siblinghood of Robbers, one only needed two reference letters from members in good standing (which Robbers Jack and Rob eagerly provided), and of course the applicant had to be in bad standing with the police.

That latter requirement was a problem for Mildred. Her occasional speeding tickets were not good enough for a rap sheet. But she was not to be deterred. With her new haircut in Maggie Thatcher style and an enormous black handbag she stormed straight into the Police Chief's office. It did not take her long to extract a bad standing letter from him. When she was done with him, he was so scared that for three full days and nights he refused to re-emerge from behind his giant filing cabinet.

Mildred's family was now in real fear that they would never see her again. They increased their ransom offer and even curbed their lawyer's passion for legal finickyness. But with a brusque "Let them stew in their own grease!" Mildred dismissed their proposal. She would not return home until her family offered substantially more than Jack's and Thyme's original demand (which would earn her a nice commission). In the meanwhile, she would run errands for the Siblinghood of Robbers, collecting protection money and other dues, which again earned her handsome commissions. She quickly gained a real reputation: her black handbag was more feared than those of the Bulgarian secret service in communist times.

Not even Robber Igor, hitherto the best debt collector of the Siblinghood, envied Mildred her success. In fact, her fame made his chores easier. A recalcitrant debtor would not want to pay? A short "All right, *tovarishch,* then Robber Mildred will take care of you!" settled the matter immediately.

CHAPTER THE TWELFTH

IN WHICH, AT AN INTERSECTION, A STALEMATE OCCURS

In the high-rise building where Robber Thyme had his apartment, there were three elevators. Thyme had never seen more than two of them in working order at the same time. The management gave the excuse that a renovation project was under way. A notice offering apologies for the temporary inconvenience was posted on every floor. It was printed on acid-free paper so that it would last long enough.

Neighbour Dennis's businesses flourished. The hot season was the best time of the year for him. With money from one of Dr Matasano's tax shelters, he had again opened a new business: Dennis' Drive-Thru Dermatology!

"Next will be Dennis' Drive-Thru Dentistry," he promised. "Get your teeth pulled in the comfort and safety of your own car!" – And the good doctor had even bigger plans. Drive-Thru Dialysis! "¡Get your blood cleaned while you keep driving around the block, with a paramedic on duty!"

"Time is not ripe yet," mused Dennis. "We can't do all kinds of medical services in drive-thru fashion. Some would not be socially acceptable." – "But the time will come," Dr Matasano assured him. "¡Wait a few years, and we will see Dennis' Drive-Thru colonoscopy! ¡And, for a very small surcharge, you will be live on TV, in a reality show!"

At the Drive-Thru Diner, they met the elderly gentleman again. Still in a long coat, but a thinner one. Still in a hurry, but very happy indeed. "This drive-thru network of yours is a true blessing for folks like me," he repeated to Dennis. – "You seem to be in a rush quite often, sir," responded Dennis. "Plenty of folks are like you, nowadays. Hence the drive-thru businesses." – "Always on the run, indeed they are! I've observed that," continued the gentleman. "Airports and highways, they're always crowded. Same with trains in such parts of the world where they care to have railways … they're always full of people on the run. Jews and *goyim*, all the same. Well, I know why I of all people need to keep moving all the time, but why would all the others?"

Before Thyme and his friends could ask for an explanation, the gentleman had driven away. Bush airport this time, he had revealed, en route to Paris, and then to Moscow. They wondered what he might carry in that time-worn black leather bag of the 'Flying Dutchman' brand.

At the Siblinghood of Robbers on the following day, the Robber Boss held an all-hands meeting. He opened it by

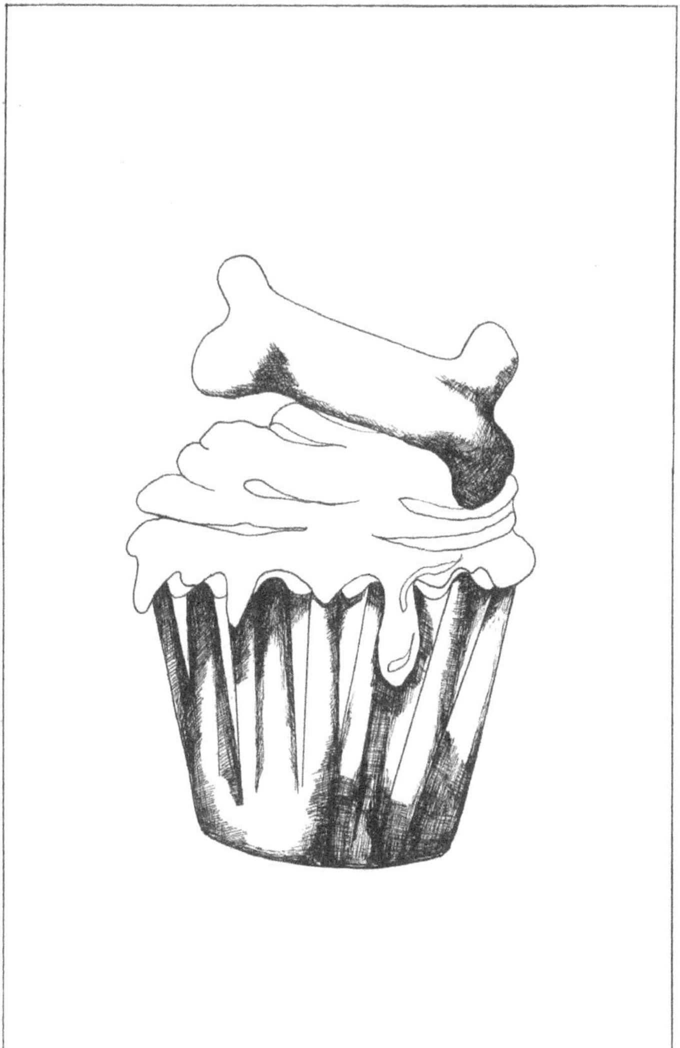

asking HR to recite a prayer (designed in such a way that all kinds of believers, and even atheists, were able to subscribe to it). Then the assembled robbers, minus some of the foreign nationals amongst them, duly pledged their allegiance to the U.S. flag and, with added emphasis, to the Texas flag. After which a speech by the Robber Boss's Big Boss was broadcast for the benefit and education of all members of the Siblinghood. A motivational speech it was, attendance mandatory. The Kingpin announced a new organisational structure, a new productivity programme, and a couple of reasons why all this was the best invention since sliced bread, or the file in a cake.

The robbers had heard this and similar speeches so often that their internal communications department had all of them numbered. "No. 17!" shouted the *capo di tutti i capi* on his screen. "Seventeen! Y'all hear me? It's the seventeen!" – "Seventeen!" repeated the local Robber Boss, and "Yeah! Seventeen!" fell in the chorus. So the meeting could be kept short, and the streets of the city did not have to stay in an unnaturally safe condition for long.

Later in the queue at the food truck (today it was soul food, procured by Robber Ezekiel), the robbers kept talking about the speech. "Seventeen's a great one, ain't it?" – "Yeah!" – *"¡La diecisiete, compadres: muy bien!"*

Freshly motivated, Robber Thyme sallied forth to burgle another villa in the West University area. Amanda the Sassy Armadillo helped him as before. It must be said though that she was quite distracted today. She listened to the police radio well enough, but failed to pass on the relevant information to Thyme.

And so, when Robber Thyme left the villa, with his booty bag well filled and himself comfortably taking a bit of snuff, what did he hear but a police siren. Thyme dropped the bag and made a run – not for his car, as the police car was approaching from that very direction, but towards the crossing on the other side. But, alas! There was another police car on the other side of the crossing. Caught between the two of them, Thyme stopped in the middle of the crossing and raised his hands.

Amanda the Armadillo was nowhere to be seen. Oh yes, there she was: sitting in one of the police cars, exchanging kisses with a police dog! Thyme missed Benedict his faithful earthworm more than ever before.

"You're under arrest!" shouted two police officers in unison, drawing their guns. But apparently this was the only matter they could agree upon. "He broke into a house in my area. I'll take the man!" yelled the one. – "He ran into my district. ¡He's mine!" hollered the other, who happened to be Hispanic. This went on for quite a while.

Robber Thyme studied the two patrol cars. West University Police said the one in which Amanda and the dog were having a good time, Houston Police Department, the other. Realising that this street, Bissonnet, was the border between their two areas, Thyme stayed on the centre line and waited for further developments.

The two boys in blue got louder and louder. Thyme feared their disagreement might develop into a gunfight. Then he would be caught in the crossfire.

A third patrol car appeared on the scene. Rice University Police. Its officer naturally sided with his West University colleague. But soon a fourth police car emerged: Harris County Sheriff. So there was a stalemate again.

Slowly and cautiously, his hands still raised, Robber Thyme started walking the centre line which apparently was the demarcation line between the two police districts. Two police cars on either side of the street were following him. For HPD and the sheriff's deputy it was more difficult: they had to go against traffic. But they all managed well, especially considering that they had ongoing radio conversations with their respective dispatchers and supervisors. How should they proceed, or how could they get support for their side from an additional police body? University of Houston Police? The Constable, Precinct No. 5? The Texas Rangers? Not the FBI, on that they could all agree.

Thyme walked on and on until a shrill shout from Amanda stopped him in his track: "¡Freeze! ¡West U area ends here!" Did her bad conscience plague her? No, probably she just sided with that police body to which her new lover the dog belonged. – "¿New?" she justified herself.

"¡I've admired him secretly for weeks! ¡Now this is the first opportunity I had to actually meet him!" – "With me as the dowrrry," complained Robber Thyme. – "¡Can't help it, baby! ¡I'm in love! ¡Really! ¡Never happened to me before!"

Thyme's arms had become heavy. How long would the stalemate last? Hope was renewed when one police officer announced his shift would end in five minutes. But, to Thyme's dismay, his relief appeared on time.

"Gentlemen! This cannot last forrreverrr." Robber Thyme addressed his non-aligned captors. "Shall I toss a coin for who is going to arrrrrrest me?" – "Don't move!" The four boys in blue were quick to agree on that. "Keep your hands up, or we'll shoot!"

"What do yourrr rrregulations say?" Thyme tried next. That was not a wise move. Each of the four quoted a different regulation, and found a different interpretation for the rule the previous one had referred to.

"I'm hungrrry!" Thyme vented then. – Houston's finest are no brutes. They called a pizza service for him. Thyme was grateful, although it was not exactly easy to eat a pizza, and to pay for it first, with your hands raised.

Amanda had spent her time in a most enjoyable manner on the back seat of the police car. But now her mood changed, and she got gloomy. *(Omne animal triste post coitum.)* Should Robber Thyme really rot in the dungeon, all because of her?

She threw another irresistible glance at the police dog. "Willie ... sing a song for me. Something romantic." – "Romantic?" retorted Willie. "I'm a police dog on duty. I can do patriotic songs only." – "¿Really?" Amanda made a show of being surprised. "¡Then sing the Star-Spangled Banner for me!"

For that she did not have to ask twice. "Wo-ow, say, can you see ..." howled Willie the police dog, Amanda the Sassy Armadillo fell in, and the four police officers had no other choice but to stand at attention and salute. For which purpose they had to holster their guns first, for otherwise, where would they point!

Thyme threw an admiring glance at Amanda. And he was grateful that no Texas Ranger was on the scene. He was not absolutely sure, but he suspected that they would holster their weapon and salute only for 'Texas, Our Texas.'

Still smiling at Amanda, Thyme started moving away from the centre stripe, in the direction where he had left his booty bag and car. But alas! An instant later he sat, minus his belt with the two pistols and the three knives, handcuffed in the back of the West U police car. The Rice University police officer had thrown him in there, next to Willie and Amanda. – "¡How could you!" yelled Amanda. – "¡How dare you!" shouted the HPD police officer and the sheriff's deputy. – The West U policeman, beaming, hardly believed his good luck.

"We have a regulation," explained a broadly grinning Rice policeman. "We have dispensation from saluting if there's a disturbance of public order. Old rule ... my father told me about it. Not used very much now, but it was back in 1968."

"Only reason to stop saluting," he assured himself. "Only other reason: cop in danger." – "¿Disturbance of public order, where did you see that here?" Amanda tried to build a case. – "This robber guy here. Ain't respectin' the national anthem. That's disturbance well enough. Same as in '68."

"That does not mean that *you* can arrest him," the Houston Police Department officer tried to interfere. "¿He ran to my side, you understand? ¡He's mine!" – "You lost, man!" the Rice U policeman insisted. "His right hand which he didn't place on his heart, did y'all see that? His right hand which he didn't use to remove his hat ... that right hand was on the West U side of Bissonnet Street all the time. And so is the whole man now!"

At Rice University, not only the students but also the police officers get a fair share of dialectics. "There's only one police body in all of Texas who can beat us at that ... occasionally. The St Thomas of Aquinas University Police."

It appeared though that speaking of the devil has its risks, even if the opposite faculty is concerned. For indeed now a fifth patrol car appeared on the scene, carrying none other but a St Thomas policeman. *"Ave Maria purissima!"* he greeted his colleagues. – "¡She has conceived without sin!" responded the two Hispanics amongst them.

The newcomer had the situation explained to him. He insisted that Thyme would get out of the car and resume his old position on the centre line, hands raised again, this time handcuffed. "So it was you who arrested him?" he asked. – "Yes! His right arm which gave the offence was on my side." – "How d'y'all know he's right-handed?" asked the St Thomas policeman. – "He sure is! I saw that when he was still carrying his booty bag." – "Inconclusive evidence!"

One might have expected that the St Thomas University policeman would side with his University colleagues. But not at all! He held Rice University in uttermost contempt for being a den of god-defying liberals. "In fact it doesn't even matter if you know he's right-handed or just assumed it. If you build your arrest on his right hand, that's unlawful discrimination!"

"¿So I can have him?" ventured the HPD officer. – "You don't have a case either," dismissed him the disciple of St Thomas of Aquinas. "I'll take him. Our Father Inquisitor has the right way of dealing with this kind of problem." Triumphantly he looked around. "Y'all told me he was standing right in the middle. I'll take him." – "How

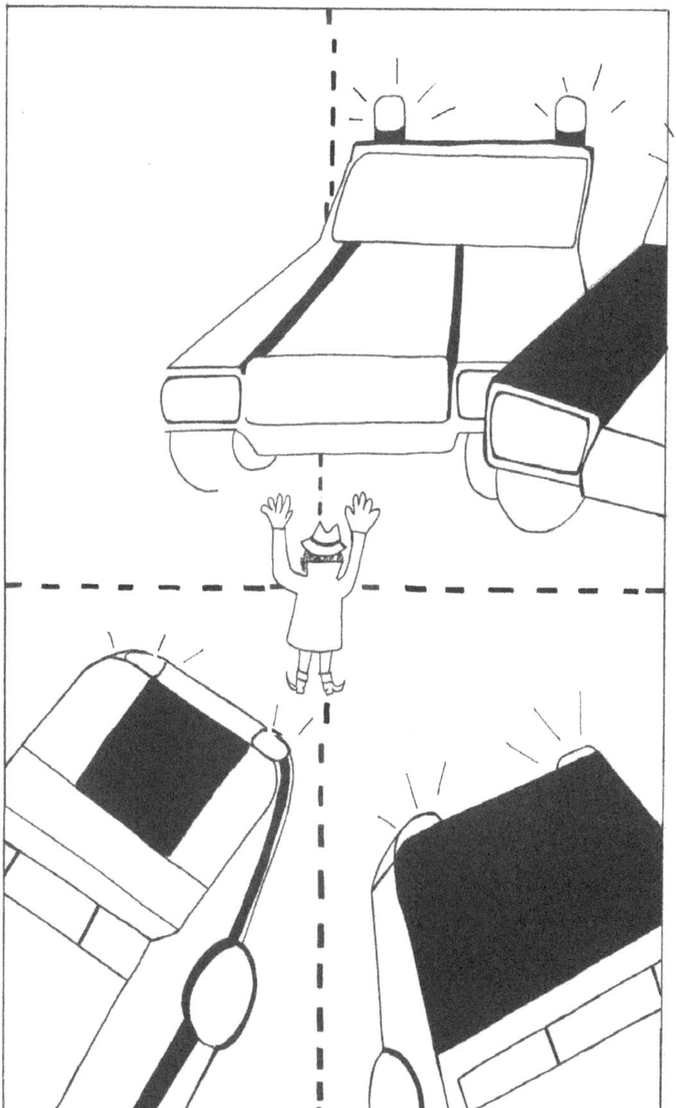

many angels can dance on the head of a pin?" commented Robber Thyme.

Which is a question so complex and serious that this true account will not be continued until the next chapter.

CHAPTER THE THIRTEENTH

IN WHICH, TO SATISFY THE READER'S ALLEGED CURIOSITY, THE PREVIOUS CHAPTER IS CONTINUED

The esteemed reader might by now entertain fears that the stalemate at the intersection would continue until Kingdom come. Indeed Robber Thyme had exactly the same apprehension. But, lo and behold, another police car appeared on the scene. "He's mine!" shouted the police officer who was sitting in it. The other boys in blue wanted to argue their cases. But look who was getting out of the newly-arrived patrol car. It was none other than Robber Rob, in a speckless police uniform, ostentatiously admiring his equally speckless assault rifle. "He's one of our students. The Provost of our Academy will take care of him, buddies. He hasn't paid his library overdues!" The other police officers cast shy looks at their own weaponry. They had handguns only, plus three rosaries. So they conceded to Rob's superior arguments.

"Höhöhö," made Robber Thyme when he sat in the back seat with Robber Rob. "Now would you please rrremove these handcuffs. They arrre awfully tight." – "First you have to see the provost marshal, buddy," said Robber Rob. "He'll decide what to do." – "Librrrarrry overrrdues, eh? That was a smarrrt move to get me out of therrre!" It was Amanda the Armadillo who deserved the kudos for that. Conscience-ridden, she had managed to broadcast on the police radio that Robber Thyme was about to be arrested.

"About to be? You are factually arrested, buddy!" stated Robber Rob. – "All rrright, let's play the show to the end!" remarked Robber Thyme. He was confident that Rob and his mate would take him to the Siblinghood and release him there. Indeed the patrol car arrived in front of that well-known building on Richmond Avenue. Now they were in front of Peter the doorman. "How are you?" – "Fine!" – "To the dungeons? Good. Out of the door. Line on the left. One cell each. Next!"

A more than astonished Thyme was thrown into a cell. Once again he pointed out his handcuffs to Robber Rob, but to no avail. – "Tell the provost marshal, buddy!" was all he got. There he sat in the company of a few robbers who had violated some of the Siblinghood's ordinances. Swearing in front of customers was a common offence. Then there were a few freelancers, caught red-handed without a robbery licence issued by the Siblinghood or one of its accredited partner organisations. These latter ones had scary appearances – no dress code, nothing.

A good couple of hours later, Robber Thyme was admitted into the presence of the provost marshal. He tried to express his indignation at being handcuffed and gaoled by the Siblinghood of Robbers whose very guest he was. The provost was unmoved: "We can return you to the Houston Police Department, if you insist, fella! Just sign this form here." – "I insist that you rrrelease me rrright now!" thundered Robber Thyme. "Who arrre you that you darrre to incarrrcerrrate an honest rrrobberrr?" – "Who I am? They didn't tell you, fella? I'm the Provost Marshal of the Siblinghood's *Interfaith and Intercultural St Dismas, Robin Hood, El Maragato, Thief of Bagdad, Tajōmaru, Outlaws of the Marsh As Well As United Thugs and Dacoits (the Sequence Implying No Preference) Academy of Advanced Robbery.* We have our own police force, as every institution of higher education has here in the States. You have certainly noticed the writing on the car, and my officers' badges." – "Rrrobberrr Rrrob, a copper? Thunderrr and Dorrria." – "Every licensed robber must take their turn. Foreign guests not exempted if staying for more than twelve months."

"So what will you do with me? You know verrry well that I have no overrrdues at yourrr librrrarrry." – "You should read, fella. Widens your horizon!" – "I am in the habit of rrreading," insisted Robber Thyme, "but not of borrrrrrowed books! Considerrr my rrreputation, prrrovost! When I crrrave to rrread, I rrrob a book at the storrre!" – "A very laudable habit, good man! But you need to confirm that we have a rightful charge against you. Otherwise we must return you to the Houston Police Department. Four seventy-five, that's all the overdues you have." – "All rrright, rrremove the handcuffs so that I can rrreach my money pouch." – "No cash, fella, credit cards only.

You won't have enough cash anyway, good man, considering the administrative fees you have got to pay." – "Administrrrative fees? Not fourrr dollarrrs seventy-five cents in overrrdues, but fourrr hundrrred seventy-five dollarrrs including the fees? That's purrre daylight rrrobberrry!" exclaimed Robber Thyme. – "That's why we are here, fella!" asserted the provost marshal. "High fees help the Siblinghood keep their membership dues at an acceptable level!"

Back home in his high-rise building, tired (and broke) after his ordeal, Robber Thyme noticed heavy snoring originating from that elevator cabin which was out of order. He walked over to notify the building management. "Yes, sir, indeed!" explained a broadly grinning building manager. "We want to ensure that our residents get the best service ever, so we have arranged for the elevator company to keep a technician here on site 24/7!"

The next morning, Robber Thyme had the opportunity to meet the service technician. A middle-aged Hispanic, evidently enjoying the bachelor's apartment into which the building management had converted the third elevator cabin, complete with bed, shower, microwave and TV set. "¡When I get promoted, *señor*, they promised me: they give me another elevator cabin so that I can bring my family!"

CHAPTER THE FOURTEENTH

IN WHICH ANOTHER BUSINESS MODEL IS DEVELOPED, AND A PUBLIC HOLIDAY IS CELEBRATED, THOUGH NOT BY EVERYONE

"No offence, buddy!" Robber Rob, plainclothed again, tried to produce a grin when he encountered Robber Thyme the next day. – "My dearrr frrriend!" responded Thyme. "Dearrrerrr than any expensive enemy!" – "Never you mind, buddy. Still better than if the City of Houston flatfoots take you. Takes far more time and money to get you out of their dungeons, buddy!"

To soften Thyme's feelings, Rob took him out for dinner that night. Robber Mildred and Dr Matasano joined in. The scene was of course one of Dennis's places, the Drive-Thru Didgeridoo, with Australian food, beer and music. All authentic, vouchsafed Dennis the Slovak, supported by the assertive nods of all his Hispanic cooks and waiters.

Dr Matasano related that, like most of his Houston colleagues, he was doing more cosmetic surgeries than anything else. That was a real hype among fashionable ladies (and are there any other?). Robber Mildred could not agree more: "Listen pards. In my circles, no marriage contract is concluded without specifying how much he has to pay for her cosmetic surgeries." – *"Per annum,"* agreed the doctor. – "I can't imagine," added Mildred, "how those poor females survive whose husbands cannot pay for some decent beauty surgery at least every other year. Not that I know such poor people, but their plight must be most horrible indeed!"

Robber Thyme mused what Mildred's social acquaintances would do if fate (or the Siblinghood) stripped them of the funds for their plastic surgeries. – "Many of my best friends would rather commit the worst felonies than to suffer that!" stated Mildred. – "That can be arranged, my dearie!" asserted Robber Rob.

For a couple of days, Rob and Mildred were exempted from their regular duties. Instead, they spent many hours in consultation with Dr Matasano and with Robber Jack's PA. The latter shaped a business model, complete with assumptions, milestones, options, and sensitivity analyses that would make his professors proud – and Texas Christian University's Jesse James School of Banking and Other Robbery is known for its high standards. (They offer programmes in cooperation with Texas ATM University where banksters and gangsters are studying side by side. Only Harvard is better, and maybe Gaol University.) The Robber Boss, on being presented the model, gave green light. "With this model, you'll be earning your spurs soon enough, son!" He slapped the PA's shoulder. "Your next car will be a regular pick-up!"

From now on, whenever members of the Siblinghood had a difficult task that their colleagues were reluctant to help them with for fear of being exposed to the police, Robber Mildred would come to the rescue. She would approach one of the countless women who had left Dr Matasano's practice in tears because they could not afford the humongous fee for his services. The task being accomplished, the surgery would be scheduled instantly, courtesy of the Brotherhood.

But how would the police force react? "Better safe than sorry!" stated Robber Rob, and offered to pay some intimidating visits to potential witnesses. The PA suggested that more ladies of the penniless sort could be encouraged in a similar manner to provide alibis by the dozen. But there was no need for that, since the police never ever interrogated any of the ladies who contributed to the new business model. The robbers did not know why. But they accepted the failure of the law enforcement agencies with grace.

Soon all of them had something else on their mind. The Fourth of July was approaching. The robbers discussed where they could watch the best fireworks: downtown, in Hermann Park, or at Clear Lake. Only one robber displayed a sour countenance in these days: John B the Englishman. He did not quite agree with the idea of American independence. "You should have stayed with King

George," he told everyone, "then you wouldn't have to complain about President Obama today!"

John B talked to the owner of the Very British Shoppe in Rice Village: would he remain open on that day, to defy history? – No, he said, and he had prepared a sign: *'Closed due to circumstances beyond our control.'*

A circular from HR wished every robber a happy holiday, reminding them not to rob a fellow-citizen on the Fourth of July, as that would be unpatriotic. – "Fellow-citizens, my foot!" burst out John B. But all of a sudden he beamed with delight. He went to the Siblinghood's armoury, grabbed as many rounds of ammunition as his belt and pockets would hold, and sallied forth to a full day of robbery with absolutely no competition. "I'm telling you, you should have stayed with King George!" he admonished every single customer on that day.

Due to the new business model, Robber Mildred's standing at the Siblinghood had increased exponentially. She was allowed to retain her personal shopper as PA. It was ever so impressive when he followed her, carrying that notorious handbag.

In a like manner, the doctor's business flourished. He had expanded his practice and threw a big inauguration party. Dennis' Drive-Thru Danish Pastries undertook the catering. Every pastry box included an ad for Dennis' Drive-Thru Dentistry.

Robbers Thyme, Rob, Jack and Mildred were there, as were Airport Eddy and Igor the debt collector. The elderly gentlemen with the goatee beard had not been able to make it. – "¡A poor sod he is, always on the run!" remarked Dr Matasano. – "I wonder whether he's been like this for all his life," said Robber Mildred. – "He must have visited many countries," Robber Rob threw in. "How many languages does he speak?" – "His Russian is excellent," contributed Robber Igor. "A bit old-fashioned, though. He told me he used to be a sleeping car attendant on the Trans-Siberian Railway. Best time of his life, he assured me. Always in motion. But he had to leave the country in 1953." – "Then he is even olderrr than I thought," mused Robber Thyme. "In quite a good shape he is forrr such an age." – "A rolling stone gathers no moss," remarked Airport Eddy.

– "Once I venturrred to ask him," confessed Robber Thyme. "I inquirrred whetherrr he had been living like this forrr decades.' – 'Decades?' he had answerrred with a bitterrr laugh. 'Nay, sir, for centuries!' – And then, as all of you can imagine, he was off to the airrrport again."

A police officer entered. The members of the Siblinghood all made inconspicuous gestures to bring their hands in closer proximity to their guns, but it was a false alarm. The flatfoot's visit was just a token of good neighbourliness. He even chatted a bit with the robbers. He was aware of the allegations against them, but was likewise aware that there had never been any noteworthy evidence against them.

Thyme decided to satisfy his curiosity. Why were there no more 'Wanted' posters in the streets, he asked the flatfoot. – "You must be from Europe, robber-sir", laughed Houston's finest. "In a city where nobody ever walks, what's the use of a street poster!" – Robber Rob explained that there were more than enough photos of wanted brethren on the Internet. – "But no females!" exclaimed Robber Thyme. "At least none overrr thirrrty." – "That's Southern chivalry!" Robber Rob fell in. – Robber Thyme was not satisfied: "Isn't that discrrrimination?" – "Certainly we don't discriminate, robber-sir," explained the policeman. "The city could never afford the punitive damages. It's all for proven practical reasons!"

Robber Thyme wondered what practical reasons these could be. Admittedly, it would be undesirable to fill the city gaol with a bunch of creatures that, outside the realm of Southern chivalry, are commonly referred to as old hags (present company excluded). But would the police rather tolerate crime?

"Never!" the police officer insisted. "No, robber-sirs and ma'am, practical reasons indeed. No use in this city to publish 'Wanted' photos of ladies above thirty-five. No witness will ever identify them. Bless my soul, after those plastic surgeries y'all sawbones are doing, doctor-sir, all these ladies are looking absolutely alike!"

CHAPTER THE FIFTEENTH

IN WHICH THE LETTERS OF THE ALPHABET APPEAR IN A SEQUENCE NEVER BEFORE EMPLOYED IN THE HISTORY OF LITERATURE

Dennis the Slovak did not rest on his laurels. His next project was a Dennis's Dalmatian Drive-Thru. "With another franchise to follow: Dennis's Dachshund Drive-Thru! Imagine how many people want to have dogs but don't want to walk them! I mean, dog or no dog, who is ever seen walking in Houston! So they come to my place, borrow a dog, and drive with it around the block in the comfort and safety of their own car!"

"But you will need people who will actually walk the dogs frrrom time to time," said Robber Thyme. – "No problem," asserted Dennis, "I'll hire a few Hispanics. They don't mind walking … in their first couple of years here at least." – "But you'll need to examine their papers most carefully," added Dr Matasano. "Don't take any illegals. ¡When doing such an un-American activity as walking in the streets, they'll be profiled by the police all the time!"

Later that day, the whole Siblinghood was in great excitement. Robber Fabio the money forger had been arrested, and the prejudiced judge had refused to accept bail in Fabio's own banknotes. – "*Corpo di bacco*, what a *schmuck* of a judge!" exclaimed Don Pacifico the *consigliere*. He explained to every robber present that this was unconstitutional: "It's against the presumption of innocence. Robber Fabio's money has to be considered lawful currency as long as Fabio has not been convicted of money forgery. I'll get him out of jail this very afternoon."

"Chi Ting is missing as well!" stated an alarmed Robber Boss. – "The Chinese robber *shiksa*?" – "Yes! She was being trained by Robber Fabio to become his assistant in money forgery."

Within the hour it became evident that she, too, had been caught and gaoled. And in fact she had been the reason for their arrests. Instead of 'In God we trust', she had printed 'In Goods we trust' on the banknotes. – "Fabio must be devastated", said Robber Rob, "he's such a staunch Catholic." – "Don't even think about printing your Flying Spaghetti Monster on banknotes!" warned the Robber Boss.

"Why not?" demanded a stubborn Robber Rob. "We have freedom of religion. An atheist money forger cannot be forced to print 'In God we trust' on his banknotes!" – "Being Chinese, Chi Ting could verrry well be an Atheist," contributed Robber Thyme. – "I'll have Henny and Rosy check that," stated the Robber Boss. – "They have our rrreligious beliefs in the perrrsonnel files?" Robber Thyme was surprised. – "Sure they do. In order not to discriminate, we have to know what not to discriminate against. Pretty obvious, isn't it?"

Rosy and Henny came with bad news. Chi Ting was a Baptist. She even had a degree from Hong Kong Baptist University. – "So she should know how to spell God!" Robber Ezekiel fell in. - "*Porca miseria!*" cursed Don Pacifico the *consigliere*. "But the Chinese *shiksa* can still use the defense of being dyslexic," he added. "If she is mentally, physically or lexically challenged, it cannot be used against her."

Off he went to see the judge. – "The *consigliere* can fix just about anything for us," asserted the Robber Boss. "We call him Don Pacifico. In other circles he's known as Reb Shlomo. Both mean the same. Father's Sicilian, mother's a Jew from New York. That's the best mixture you can get if you want to breed lawyers ... Not that I would want to discriminate," he added hastily.

The robbers returned to their cubicles, shuffling their paperwork until the *consigliere* returned. To distract himself, Robber Thyme talked with Robber Jack's PA about a new business idea for Dennis: a Drive-Thru Dormitory. Many students would come to college with their parents' old cars. Being Texans, their cars were usually large enough to fit in a few pieces of furniture. Well, the shower might be a bit of a problem, but a refrigerator, a microwave and Internet access could be accommodated easily enough. "And then we'll put these carrrs on a conveyerrr and let them rrrun arrround the block all night," said Robber

Thyme. – "And, for a very small surcharge, their car will be gently rocked," added the PA, "so that the poor freshmen get over their homesickness."

Don Pacifico returned. The robbers had never seen him in such agitation before. All his arguments about prejudice and discrimination had been refuted. Instead, the biased judge had used another instrument against Fabio and Chi Ting – copyright law!

"So, if you pay a licence fee to the Federrral Rrreserrrve System, you may prrrint as many dollarrr notes as you want?" Curious as always, Robber Thyme tried to understand the American reasoning. – "That's a fact, shipmate," confirmed Robber Jack. "But they charge such an outrageous license fee that there's no point in sailing that course!" – "Isn't that an unlawful impediment to frrree enterrrprrrise?" Robber Thyme had obviously done his homework. – *"È vero,"* confirmed the *consigliere*, "but the judges that hear cases like this are such *golems*. They have no idea about the finesses of anti-trust law!"

Nothing could be done before the next hearing. In low spirits, Thyme and Robber Jack went out to have dinner with Dr Matasano. *Dennis' Drive-Thru Al Dente Spaghetteria*, this time. As was to be expected, not much time passed before the elderly gentleman with the grey goatee beard joined them in an adjacent car. They heard him talking on his cellphone, apparently about the space programme. "Maybe he is a lobbyist," remarked the doctor.

Suddenly there was noise and disruption. One of the waiters apparently had a dispute with another guest, and then with his manager. He ran to his car, returned with a gun, and shot indiscriminately at guests and staff alike. – "A lousy shot," Robber Jack coolly remarked. "Must be a foreigner, and a landlubber on top. I don't understand why there's not a proper shooting test before they give such folks a work visa."

It was a surreal sight, the chef throwing pots and pans at the waiter with the pistol. But suddenly it was no longer funny. With his last bullet, whirling around before being knocked out by a casserole with *ossobuco*, he shot the bearded gentleman straight through the heart.

Robber Thyme was shocked. "A thing like that just cannot happen in a book like this," he howled. "What will the Tomcat say, the Tomcat who tells Fairrry-Tales?" – Most of the other guests were not distressed. Nor was Robber Jack: "This is Texas, shipmate. We mind very much being stabbed in the back. That's what the Mexicans do. No discrimination, but we just don't like that. On the other hand, a shot from the front, that's fair and square. Nobody in their right mind can object to that. Savvy?"

"Listen, a man was shot herrre in frrront of ourrr verrry eyes!" insisted Thyme. "A man whom we all knew!" – "Come on, he was not even sailing on our ship. Savvy? Listen: if you cry your eyes out over every Jack Tar that makes it for Davy Jones' locker, you'll never become a decent pirate!" – Thyme insisted on his feelings. – "What's wrong with you, shipmate?" inquired Robber Jack. "All monsters of the seven seas! Can't we have a little gunplay every now and then? You're not one of those godforsaken liberals, are you?" – Robber Thyme did not know what to say. – Dr Matasano tried to calm the waves: "He's European, they're different," he explained.

"Doctorrr!" shouted Robber Thyme, "do something!" – "No need to interrupt my dinner," retorted Dr Matasano. "¡With a hit like that, the man is as dead as downtown Houston on a Sunday afternoon in August!" – "How can you be so indifferrrent!" Thyme was now seriously taken aback.

The Hispanic staff assembled around the gentleman, placed his ten-gallon hat over his eyes and wished *Su Eternidad* a good rest. The manager called the police. Since the victim was already dead, and the assassin was already knocked out and secured, the police dispatcher saw no reason to classify this as an emergency. Within the next hour or two an officer would arrive on site, and please don't touch anything until then, thanks very much.

Jack and the Doctor finished their dinner in all tranquillity, even had coffee afterwards. Thyme had lost his appetite. The manager casually remarked that a curious waiter had unveiled the secret of the gentleman's time-worn black leather bag. He had carried some very old-fashioned shoemaker's tools in it, with a very modern book on how to survive in the absence of gravity, *Jesucristo* knows why. Dr Matasano speculated whether Dennis had already created a business for life events like this, the Drive-Thru Funeral Home?

Suddenly they realised that the murdered gentleman's car was gone. Nobody had removed the corpse from the car, they were certain about that. Who would steal a car with a dead body in the driver's seat?

Broken-hearted and unable to sleep, Robber Thyme tossed and turned in his bed. He had sent an SMS to the Tomcat Who Tells Fairy-Tales. In the small hours, the answer arrived: "Wait for the next chapter."

CHAPTER THE SIXTEENTH

IN WHICH THE FOLLOWING DAY IS DESCRIBED

The next morning came. No further communication from the Tomcat Who Tells Fairy-Tales. Robber Thyme, downcast and dreary, drove over to the Siblinghood in order to get an update on the fate of Fabio and Chi Ting. No news on them either. Instead, he was once again cornered by Rosy and Henny. Today they were sporting antebellum New Orleans dresses.

"You need to drive home again and don your *Lederhose*," they urged him. "It's Ethnic Heritage Day!" – Thyme tried to explain to them that in his part of Germany no-one would wear a *Lederhose*. His arguments were lost on the HR ladies. Fortunately they had no more time for him. – "Hey, just to please you: I'll have a *Brrratwurrrst* forrr lunch!" he shouted after them.

Soon thereafter a loudspeaker announcement ordered all robbers into the big meeting room. There was the Robber Boss on stage, with Henny and Rosy. Prayer, pledge of allegiance to the U.S. flag, same (with greater emphasis) to the Texas flag. Then bow-legged Robber Raoúl was asked to come up on stage. In his black suit he looked more dapper than ever. The Robber Boss announced that Raoúl was hereby awarded the Siblinghood's Golden Heritage Award, which was a little sculpture, plus a free trip to Las Vegas, including a full day of exclusive pickpocketing at one of the world's best casinos – for having developed a business model that combined the best of his heritage with the vision and mission of the Siblinghood, yeah!

When the applause had faded, a video was shown to the assembled robbers. It showed a *Quinceañera*, the ceremonial fifteenth birthday of a Mexican girl. "His daughterrr?" asked Robber Thyme. He had seen photo shoots for this kind of festivity at the fountains in the street where he lived. – "Shhhhh!" hissed the others.

The video continued with the *fiesta* itself. The guests had all assembled. The ladies were dressed in colours as loud as in the first years of Technicolor movies. The birthday girl made her grand entrance, then danced the first waltz with her father. The males of her honour guard followed, the chamberlains. They waltzed through the hall into the lush garden. Again, Thyme recognised the location: an events facility in *hacienda* style right in his neighbourhood called the *Parador*. But, like most robbers present, he still did not know what the film was all about.

Then something unforeseen happed. A rider appeared on a black horse, clad all in black: suit, cloak, hat and mask. "Zorro!" shouted the guests in unison. In fact it was none other than Robber Raoúl! And this time he was indeed on horseback. He cracked his whip in all points of the compass, then grabbed the girl and lifted her in front of him unto the saddle. Fortunately the horse was TX XL, for so was the girl. Raoúl saluted ceremoniously to the girl's parents, then galloped off, to thundering applause from the guests – and from the robbers in the auditorium.

"It's all pre-arranged," said Robber Raoúl with a smile of false modesty. "The family pays a handsome fee, and the girl has an extravagant adventure to mark her passage to adult life." – "Sounds morrre like an acting job than like honest rrrobberrry!" Robber Thyme could not keep from saying. A few other robbers of the more traditional kind seemed to have similar misgivings. Robber Raoúl, on stage, felt that he was in danger of losing rapport with his audience.

"¡Don't worry, my friends!" he exclaimed. "There's enough honest work in it. I talked everything through with the *consigliere*. I do a little marriage swindle with each of the girls. They enjoy it, and I'm on the right side of our statutes."

Robber Raoúl had even enhanced his business model: "The family … we ask them beforehand which relatives they don't care for too much but have to invite anyway for decorum. Then I'll have a few of our *compadres* amongst the waiters and guests. They'll take care of these people's wallets." – "Steal them?" Henny-or-Rosy gave the cue. – "¡You bet!" Raoúl carried on. "¡Or, for a small surcharge, we'll replace their wallets with an identical one that has only forged money in it. ¡Very embarrassing for them!"

The traditionalists amongst the robbers were satisfied. And indeed everybody had to admire Raoúl's horsemanship. Thyme took another pinch of snuff. The Robber Boss encouraged everybody to follow Raoúl's example and to compete for the Golden Heritage Award next year. Robber Thyme wondered whether he could bring in Jakob the Elephant, his old friend and partner in crime. He would not mind doing a few abductions on elephant-back in Houston's Indian quarter, the Gandhi District.

Or perhaps team up with a dragon and take on Chinatown? Houston's Chinese population would be duly impressed. They were well established there – even the district's police station had a sign with Chinese characters. *'No wrongdoings here unless you have the right guanxi,'* the text said. But Thyme could not read the sign, and Chi Ting was not here to tell him.

Chi Ting. There were still no news of her, nor of Robber Fabio. When the award ceremony was over, Thyme could not endure sitting still. He went to a nearby parking garage, intending to rob a couple of people at gunpoint. But, alas!, after that sleepless night he had forgotten to reload his two pistols after cleaning. He still had his three knives, but he felt they might not be convincing enough for the clientele he would encounter.

Fortunately, as we already had occasion to observe, Houston is inhabited by a bunch of really friendly people. The garage customer whom Robber Thyme asked had no ammo of the right calibre. But he didn't mind lending his gun to Thyme for a few hold-ups. "Just give it back to the garage attendant when you're done, chum! Tell him it's mine ... Raymond's the name."

Loaded with booty, Robber Thyme returned home. He did not have much of an appetite, but Dr Matasano took him out for dinner. "Doctor's orders," he insisted. And all of a sudden, while a listless Thyme pretended to work on his Texas-sized burger, there appeared – the elderly gentleman with the coat and the goatee beard. The very one whom they had seen shot in the heart the evening before.

Dr Matasano made the sign of the cross, over and over again. The bearded gentleman did not really appreciate that gesture: "I've had enough trouble with that in my time," he explained. – "But ... but ... arrren't you ..." stuttered Robber Thyme, pointing at the hole in the windshield of the bearded gentleman's car. – "Dead? Not me. Had a bit of a heartache, yes. I'm not above that, I have to admit. *Aber man lebt!*" – "¡*Madre de dios!*" the doctor burst out (again the elderly gentleman winced). "¡*Jesucristo*, this is a medical impossibility!"

"What do you know ... what do you *goyim* know about me ... and about that Jesus and his *mame*," said the elderly gentleman melancholically. "All these things that happened so long ago. Listen, young man: if a *meshuggener* could kill me just so *ain-tswai-drai*, I would have kicked the bucket before you were even born. In fact," he added, "not even you and all your sawbones-*chawerim* at the medical centre over there could kill me. And that's saying something! But now you will kindly excuse me, I have a plane to catch. Important meeting in Washington." Thus spoke the elderly gentleman to an astonished audience.

Minus the Hispanic staff, that is. They were not in the least surprised. "We always knew that we would see *Su Eternidad* again," they insisted. Thyme was puzzled but relieved.

CHAPTER THE SEVENTEENTH

IN WHICH THE SUPERIORITY OF THE JURY SYSTEM IS EXEMPLIFIED

The next day at the Siblinghood, there was Amanda the Sassy Armadillo whom Robber Thyme could thank for both his arrest and his expensive liberation. She greeted him with a shy smile. – "How's Willie the police dog?" he inquired. – "He wants me to go over to his side, baby," she said. "Cut all ties to the Siblinghood, he insists. ¿What can I do?" – "Sail back to Mexico," Robber Jack suggested unfeelingly. – "¡No more of that nonsense!" Amanda protested. "¡Armadillo may sound Spanish, but I am as much a Texan as anyone else here! ¡In fact, my folks were settled and established here many decades before yours ever bought their steerage tickets and became seasick!"

"Therrre comes the *consiglierrre*." Robber Thyme tried to steer the conversation away from the minefield of historic sensitivities. – *"Mascalzone! Birbone! Furfante!"* Don Pacifico cursed more than ever. "That judge is such a *mamzer*, he refused bail even for real money." – "So what will happen next?" Thyme demanded to know. – "They will go on trial. A jury will be formed."

At Thyme's request, Don Pacifico elaborated on how the jury system works. All the robbers joined him in praising

the U.S. legal system, where everyone is tried by a jury of their peers. – "¿What does that mean?" inquired Amanda the Armadillo. "¿If I'm accused in court, will they have to form a jury of armadillos?" – "It doesn't work that way," explained Robber Rob. "A black guy won't get an all-black jury, nor a female an all-female one."

"¿So what is it all about?" insisted Amanda. "¿How can they be my peers if there is not a single armadillo among them?" – "You can bet there won't be an armadillo in the jury pool," laughed Robber Jack. "But don't worry, they'll hang you from the yardarm anyway."

On hearing this exchange, Don Pacifico dropped his pen, and his jaws hit the floor. Neither of which had happened since grad school. "Jury pool … it's unconstitutional." He bowed down and kissed Amanda. "*Benissimo!* You think like a *yiddisher kop!*" – The robbers had never before seen an armadillo turning red, let alone a sassy one. – "It won't be a fair trial," the *consigliere* continued, "if there is not a money forger in the jury pool. I can get any verdict overturned on that basis."

While Don Pacifico rushed back to the court to gather more data on the jury pool, the robbers discussed Amanda's future outside the Siblinghood. Could she find work as a bodyguard? Or with an armoured car service? – "You could give us a valuable cue every now and then," suggested Robber Rob. – "So sorry. ¡No more work for the Siblinghood, that's what Willie says, baby!"

With a heavy heart, Amanda turned in her membership card. The Robber Boss and the *consigliere* mustered Thyme and a few others to take her out to lunch one last time. Even Robber Jack was sad. "I'll miss bickering with you, pirate queen," he acknowledged.

On their way to the restaurant they passed Dennis's latest establishment: his Drive-Thru Diaper Change Service. – "Hi there, friends!" Dennis waved at them. *"Pecunia non olet!"* A billboard informed an esteemed clientele that babies were welcome 24/7, while a lane for adult incontinence would open next month.

"What will come next?" wondered the robbers. – "Culture?" suggested Robber Thyme. "A drrrive-through museum wherrre the paintings will be passed thrrrough frrrom one carrr to anotherrr." – "No way," retorted Dennis, "lousy cash-flow. I need to offer something where tons of people will come." – "A drive-thru fitness studio!" the *consigliere* burst out. "Do your *goyim naches* exercise in the comfort and safety of your own car!" – Dennis admitted he had already thought of that, given the immense popularity of fitness studios in the land of unlimited car-driving. "Have to solve the shower problem first," he added sadly.

Amanda asked Dennis forthrightly: "¿Do you have a job for me? I have to turn honest." – Dennis scratched his head: "Never thought of employing an armadillo. But why not!" They all drove over to Dennis's Drive-Thru Beijing Duck Diner where the interview would continue.

Not at all easy to eat Beijing Duck in a car. But Dennis would not care. "Good for my Drive-Thru Dry-Cleaning!" he chuckled.

"Do you have references?" Dennis asked Amanda. – "¡They're sitting all around me here!" asserted Amanda. – With the Robber Boss and the *consigliere* being part of the crowd, Dennis was satisfied indeed. "You're not in a trade union, are you? All right, you can start tomorrow with the lunch shift!"

So Amanda the Sassy Armadillo was provided for. Now Robber Rob had a request. He had spotted Dr Matasano in one of the adjacent cars. "Hey, Doc, how are you? Can you teach me some medical mumbo-jumbo? Nothing specific, I just need to impress the real estate agent with a bit of sawbones lingo when I meet her tomorrow."

The members of the Siblinghood had learned long ago that in their dealings with real estate agencies they were better off not mentioning their trade and profession. They usually pretended to have some rather uninteresting occupation to evade further questions.

Robber Rob on the other hand had developed a different strategy. Wearing upscale clothes, he would pose as a successful medical doctor. Visiting posh places in classy neighbourhoods, he would then ask the realtors for the best places to hide valuables in the house. When the place was sold and the new owners had had enough time to settle in, he would come back with the tools of his regular trade.

"That's a long shot, shipmate," said Robber Jack. "I prefer ships where we don't have to wait for captain and crew to come aboard." – "You're right, buddy," agreed Robber Rob. "In that case, my method will work even better. House is for sale, owners haven't moved out yet. Agent will tell me where to hide valuables in the house. I come back the next day and take care of them. Just teach me the right lingo, Doc."

"There's one downside of being in the medical field," commented Dr Matasano. "Everybody will tell you their symptoms and ask for advice. Free advice, mind." – "So what do I tell them, Doc?" inquired Robber Rob, "two aspirin, and half a gallon of water per day?" – "Just tell them you're an urologist," advised the good doctor, "or a specialist for venereal diseases. They'll leave you alone pretty quick."

Given the fact that this conversation was taking place at an eatery, this true account will refrain from relating further details from it, and adjourn until the next day.

On said morning, Robber Thyme was told that it was his turn today to organise the food truck for the robbers' lunch. He wanted to give his colleagues a special treat and drove up all the way to Fredericksburg. That place was boasting all over Texas with its German heritage, so they would certainly have a truckload of *Bratwurst mit Sauerkraut* for him?

Thyme enjoyed the drive through the Hill Country. But the town is a sham, he had to conclude. *Spaghetti bolognese* and Serbian bean soup was all that he could find. – "You hit the wrong place, *Kamerad*," Robber Karl-Wilhelm told him, the Siblinghood's renowned tax expert. "Go to Old Town Spring next time. *Das ist wunderbar!*"

CHAPTER THE EIGHTEENTH
WHICH HAS NO SUBTITLE BUT THIS

A few days later, Robber Thyme inquired at the Siblinghood what other animal he could cooperate with, now that Amanda the Armadillo had left their ranks. "Back home I worrrked with an eearrrthworrrm, and laterrr with an elephant," he explained. – The *consigliere* recommended a doe. Her name was Jane. Quite a celebrity, he added. "Ever suspected, never caught!" he related. "That Jane Doe ... you should see her doe eyes. Innocence in perfection! The greatest *schmuck* of a lawyer will get her cleared even if she was caught red-hoofed. If there are enough males on the jury, that is."

Robber Igor recommended a skunk like the one that accompanied him on his debt-collection rounds. "Believe me, *tovarishch*, there's nothing better than a skunk to get all those guard dogs out of your way!"

It turned out however that Jane Doe was fully booked for weeks to come, and so were the few skunks that worked for the Siblinghood. Robber Fauxbourdon (the Cajun who worked in the parks with Louis the Squirrel) said he knew an iguana, Ildefons by name. "'e is a bit 'ard of 'earing," said the Cajun, "but a very fine fellow!"

Robber Thyme wondered how a deaf iguana could stand guard for him. But he decided to give it a try. On his way home he stopped at the Beijing Duck place to get a letter of recommendation from Amanda the Armadillo. There she was, sassier than ever, proudly posing behind a sign, 'Real Chinese dragon.'

And there was Dennis, broadly grinning. "Lots of new customers come because of her. Houston Chronicle was already here. Have to hire a PR agent now to make her famous through social media. And then, the TV talk-shows!"

A few blocks down the road, Robber Thyme spotted the latest addition to his neighbour's empire: Dennis' Drive-Thru Day-care. The kids were dropped off by their parents in the morning, then driven around and around the block in brand-new vans equipped with the latest videos and computer games.

"¿What else could they want nowadays?" commented Dr Matasano, when Thyme told him over dinner what he had seen. "¡But rest assured, Dennis will tell the parents that he has a top-notch curriculum that will lead the kiddos straight into Harvard, Stanford or Rice! You have to do that nowadays. ¡You can bet he'll show them videos in Chinese!"

The next morning, Robber Thyme met the iguana in Hermann Park. Ildefons carried an enormous ear trumpet. Thyme found out that it was equipped with the latest in

audiology. – "And the best thing about it, pal," said Ildefons, "I can switch it all off. Then the guard dogs can give me their usual *spiel*, 'I'll-bite-you-I'll-maim-you-I'll-maul-you,' and I just say: ¡Louder, I can't hear you!"

"What if they rrreally bite you?" Robber Thyme was concerned. – "Don't worry, pal. Their teeth are no match for mine. Most of them know that. And the others ... they'll learn pretty fast." – Robber Thyme was impressed. They made an appointment for the next day and parted as friends.

In the afternoon, Thyme followed an invitation to a coffee party given by the kind old lady whom they had kidnapped. Naomi was delighted to see him again. There were new photos of her grandchildren by the dozen, and other photos which she was not sure whether she had shown them to him or not, and more photos still, which she was sure she had shown him but he might have forgotten by now.

More importantly, there were her friends, a group of charming Texan old ladies who had begged Naomi to introduce them to that famous robber from the Old World. They hung on his every word when he recounted how the robbers, with the help of the Texas-Size Duck, had planned and prepared for the abducktion, and how the other old lady, Mildred, had now made her way into the Siblinghood.

But even more, they liked to hear about Europe. All of them had ancestors there, and Thyme had to relate the most hideous, heinous crimes that were committed in the places whence their families had hailed from. Hearing about murderers, robbers and thieves, about dungeons, pillory and gallows gave them the most enjoyable shudders.

Thyme was a good storyteller. The old ladies were completely smitten by him. Thyme had to refuse marriage proposals by the dozen. He was determined to remain faithful to that lady with the green eyes and golden hair, who had enchanted him from a distance in the Tomcat's previous book about himself. The ladies would certainly understand, wouldn't they? – No, they would not. His romance made Thyme even more adorable to them. But Thyme did not yield.

And now he had to take his leave, there was work to do. The *kosher* cake and the company had been so good; Thyme tried to get away without robbing the ladies. But they absolutely insisted. Every single one of them declared she would be mortally offended if he didn't rob her. "At gunpoint, if you please, young man. Do it by the book!" – "All rrright, ma'ams, yourrr wish is my command."

The kiss on the hand that Robber Thyme administered after each purse he took bowled the old ladies over completely. "My friends at the temple will be green with envy when I tell them this," they assured him. Thyme was glad that his old-school habits were appreciated at last.

Then he picked up his new companion Ildefons at Hermann Park. They drove to the house that Thyme, stepping in for Chi Ting who was still in gaol, had to do next. A large sign greeted them: *'We don't call 911. And we won't send flowers.'* Another sign recommended a law office in the neighbourhood specialising in last wills, *'Make sure to visit them before you trespass here!'*

Ildefons went ahead. The two guard dogs delivered their usual litany into the iguana's ear trumpet, then retracted sulkily behind the house. Ildefons, with his teeth bared towards the dogs' hiding place, signalled to Thyme that the coast was clear.

The door was no match for Thyme's lock picks, and gave up. Thyme stepped into the house. A concrete floor again. Thyme found that uncomfortable. But he had to admit that they were more beneficial to his trade than those squeaky wooden floors.

He went straight into the master bedroom to search for jewellery. Might they be old-fashioned enough to store some cash under the mattress, or maybe a credit card? There was a chest which looked as if it might contain valuables. It had a button which Thyme pressed. But instead of a safe, only another TV set emerged.

Thyme checked the refrigerator. Some people stored their banknotes there, as if they would melt in the sun. Others hide their cash in the bathroom. Again, *pecunia non olet*.

While Thyme searched the house's three bathrooms, he suddenly heard Ildefons giving the agreed alarm signal. The iguana played the *'Yellow Rose of Texas'* on his harmonica. Not very well, this true account is obliged to record, but certainly recognisable.

Now Robber Thyme should have dashed to the garden door and run for dear life. But it is not easy to get into running mode when one is stretched and bent over to examine potential hiding places behind the toilet bowl. Thyme made it to his feet but not to the garden door, and thus was confronted by an angry homeowner. "What the hell d'you think you're doing here? You're a goddam thief and burglar, ain't you?"

Now Thyme felt at a disadvantage, since the statutes of the Siblinghood prohibited the use of swearwords on their clientele, even if provoked. "You'rrre quite rrright, sirrr," he said in his most conciliatory tone, "I'm herrre on behalf of the Siblinghood of Rrrobberrrs." – "You sound like a bloody foreigner," the unpacified homeowner observed. "Can't that goddam Siblinghood send me a proper American robber! I'm ready to support patriotic business, I always am, but my hard-earned money is not for limeys, frog-eaters, and krauts!"

"That sounds almost like discrrrimination, sirrr," remarked Robber Thyme. By now, he had turned into a real expert on that topic. – But, "I don't give a shit!" shouted the homeowner at the top of his voice. "I hate whom I want!" – Thyme had never met such antagonism amongst the friendly populace of Houston. Could this client be an uprooted native of D-town?

Be that as it may, Thyme found it appropriate to bring the discourse to a level more appropriate for an encounter in Texas. "Considerrr my arrrguments, sirrr," he whispered, pointing at the two pistols and three knives in his belt. "I guess you don't carrre to be shot by a bloody forrreignerrr, sirrr."

"No, I'll shoot you first!" fumed the homeowner. This is Texas, man! I have the whole law on my side: Stand your Ground, the Castle Doctrine … you name it, I have it!" Finally, Robber Thyme had the opportunity to prove that he had not attended classroom training in vain. "I'm afrrraid you'rrre mistaken, sirrr," he argued, still in his most gentle voice. "*I* can stand *my* grrround herrre. This is my worrrkplace. I have a licence issued by the Siblinghood. I have everrry rrright to be herrre." – "Don't provoke me any further!" shouted the homeowner, adding more expletives than this true account would care to record.

"I'm not prrrovoking you, sirrr, I'm just doing my job. In case you arrre not satisfied with the serrrvice I am prrroviding," Thyme added mischievously, "herrre's the num-

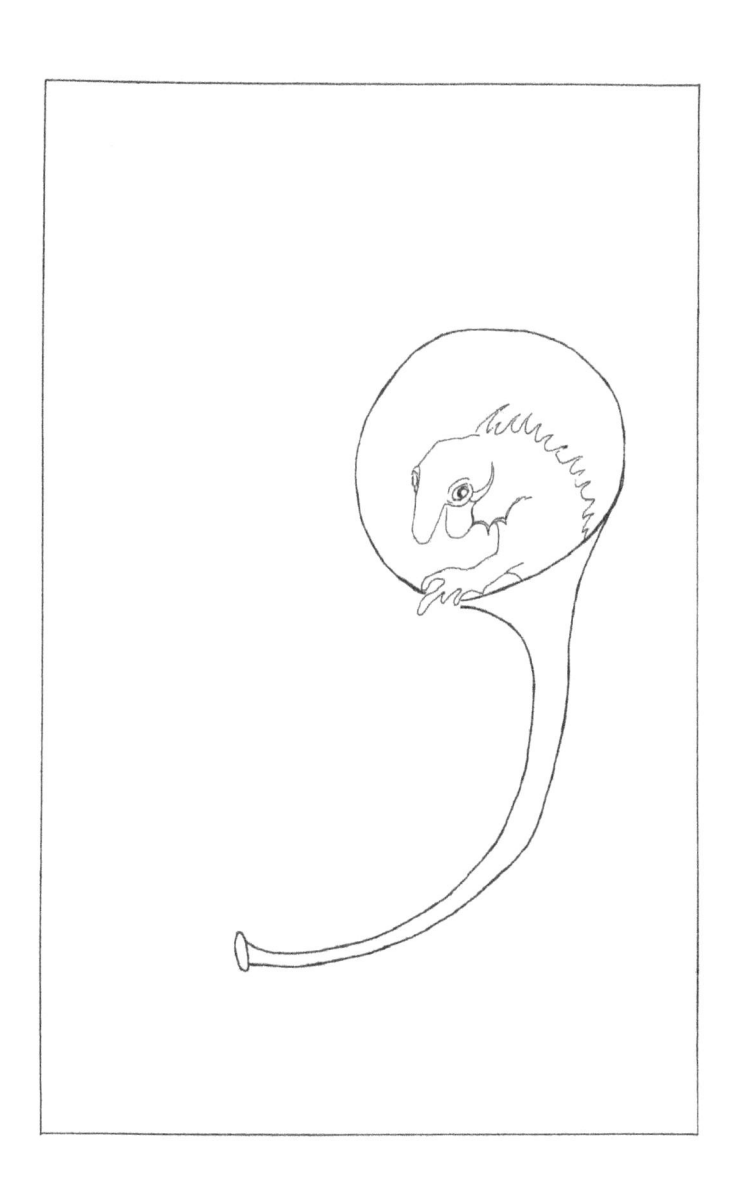

berrr of our complaints hotline. Feel frrree to call, and to listen to theirrr awful music. Besides, sirrr, would you kindly considerrr that I have my two pistols rrright herrre, wherrreas yourrr guns may be in the carrr, orrr perrrchance at the pawnbrokerrr's."

An instant later, Thyme, with a piece of chewing gum in his mouth to show his appreciation of local customs, shoved the fretting homeowner through the house, softly inquiring after the valuables that each room might contain. The jewellery was found in a gravy boat in the living room, and the cash had been hidden in an empty teapot in the kitchen. So far, so good. Now the owner insisted that he had a valuable gun collection upstairs. Wouldn't the robber-sir want to have a look at it?

Thyme was surprised how polite the homeowner had become. A triumph of his own superior diplomacy, Thyme wondered (with a glance at his pistols)? – "I have the key," trilled the homeowner, "I'll open the gun cabinet for you. Stand back, robber sir, the door is heavy."

"Don't botherrr", Thyme retorted. He was too old a hand to be fooled like that. "Now *you* stand back." Thyme had no inclination to see the gun cabinet opened, valuable pieces or not. He rather fancied a little practical joke: he thumbed his chewing gum into the lock of the gun cabinet. "Yourrr next family dispute will have to be rrresolved without a shoot-out," he told a frustrated homeowner, before retiring with the faithful iguana to one of the watering holes of Rice Village (or Noodle Village, as the older inhabitants still called it; after Nehemiah, as we know).

CHAPTER THE NINETEENTH

WHICH INTRODUCES US TO THE SPIRITUAL AND THE TEMPORAL LORD OF A GAOL

After months of merciless sun and a humidity that defied description, the first signs emerged that the summer heat was past its prime. Slowly but steadily, the city came back to life. Porches, gardens and outdoor seating areas no longer stood deserted. Joggers did not look like lobsters anymore. The parks were repopulated.

Robber Thyme did a few hold-ups in Hermann Park and on the banks of Brays Bayou. With one customer it took a little longer than expected. He was short of cash – he lacked just twelve dollars to reach the level of booty that would grant him silver status under the Siblinghood's frequent customer programme. But he had a friend in the neighbourhood from whom he could borrow that trifling amount.

Thyme promised to wait. He enjoyed his outdoor activity. And he received a lot of customer appreciation: "The robbers are back in the open! Thank God, the heat is over."

Indoor business flourished as well, since an honest robber now had a better chance of searching a home in peace without interference from homebound owners. And the water of the nearby Gulf of Mexico was still comfortably warm.

The general joy and merriment did not however extend to Robber Fabio and Chi Ting the Chinese robber girl. They were still languishing in gaol, waiting for trial. The readers of this true account should not blame the *consigliere* for that. Don Pacifico had toiled all summer. And now he received help from an unexpected corner. The Baptist prison chaplain had complained to the warden that Robber Fabio was making converts to Catholicism every week: "I don't mind them Hispanics being Catholics, or the Irish. It's not their fault, that's just how they've been brought up. But my own folks, they'd better stay away from popery!"

The prison warden did not care whether his inmates were Baptist, Catholic, or believed in the Flying Spaghetti Monster. But he agreed with the chaplain for a different reason: Fabio had the disturbing ability to find privileges and loopholes in the prison rules for every inmate who didn't mind saying a few *Ave Marias* per day.

The warden had a degree from the Law Enforcement Academy of the Lone Ranger College. But his was no match for Fabio's Jesuit-trained brain. So he agreed that keeping Robber Fabio in the prison system for years to come was a most undesirable prospect.

Considering the female prisoners' section, both chaplain and warden wanted to get rid of Chi Ting as well. The chaplain disapproved of her invitations to Buddhist prayer and meditation circles. Not that she knew a lot about Buddhism, but it proved more than enough to lead quite a few of the chaplain's black sheep astray.

The warden took even more offence at these meetings than the indignant chaplain. For he had reason to suspect that Chi Ting was in fact recruiting and training inmates for the Chinese triad whose local dragon head for Houston she was aspiring to become. So both the religious and the worldly leader wholeheartedly supported the *consigliere*'s endeavour to get Fabio and Chi Ting acquitted.

To achieve this worthy goal, Don Pacifico had dropped his earlier reliance on the presumption of innocence and chosen a different strategy. And, with a little help from the legal community, he had finally reached his goal. The trial would open next week with a true jury of peers: money forgers, art forgers and perjurers had a clear majority. Not convicted ones of course, since they would be ineligible for jury duty. But, even if undetected by the law-enforcing agencies, according to the sources of the *consigliere* they were guilty beyond reasonable doubt.

In the meanwhile, Amanda the Sassy Armadillo, a.k.a. the Real Chinese Dragon, had moved through the ranks at Dennis's Drive-Thru Beijing Duck Diner. Dennis was ready to overlook her criminal past and to make her a franchise partner. But she confessed she was not made for a conventional life. Her passion for crime was irrepressible.

The robbers were glad to reinstate her membership. Gratefully, she volunteered to reconnoitre the area of the prison where Fabio and Chi Ting languished, and to smuggle secret messages in and out. Willie the police dog would accompany her, under the pretext of patrolling the area so that no prisoner could escape.

A few days later, however, Willie was out in the street, in a dark mood, and without collar and badge. The police captain had demanded to see him. The City of West University Place had completed its annual update of mandatory background checks for all staff on its police force. And, while Willie had no problem passing the drug test, his relationship with Amanda had not gone unnoticed. As a consequence he was removed from the force.

Amanda, on learning this, was eager to get Willie into the Siblinghood. He had nothing to lose, so why not give it a try? So Robber Thyme did his next villa job accompanied by a veritable menagerie. The guard dog called all his friends so that they would not miss the spectacle. Amanda, Willie and Ildefons had a host of good stories to tell, and the German *Bratwurst* provided by Thyme contributed to the general merriment.

But the next morning Willie had a terrible hangover. His conscience troubled him. Hadn't he assured his police captain that he would never ever go over to the dark side?

– "¡It's not that you abandoned the force," Amanda tried to comfort her lover, "they kicked you out!" – He would not be consoled by her.

Thyme suggested they talk to the *consigliere*. That Sicilian New York Jewish lawyer could solve any problem, hadn't he just shown that? But Amanda said she had an even better idea. She would talk to the elderly gentleman with the goatee beard. He had been her favourite customer at Dennis's, and she was convinced that, with all his experience in life, he would tell her the right thing. "May take a while before I will see him again," she said, "but he will come back, as sure as there is a NASA in Houston."

That evening while waiting for the elevator at his home, Robber Thyme met a neighbour in a sweaty t-shirt with the text "I hiked the Great Wall of China!" – "Congratulations! That's quite an achievement, up and down all the hills over there" remarked Thyme. – "Read the small print," gasped the sportive neighbour, "it was a virtual hike." – Thyme, flabbergasted, asked for an explanation. – "Well, we register via the website, then we hike the original distance of the Great Wall back home." – "What?" – "Yes! That's how it works! We even get DVD's which we can watch while hiking in the comfort and safety of our treadmill here in our own building!" – Thyme understood why the Tomcat Who Tells Fairy-Tales finds it increasingly difficult to invent absurdities in his stories. Every so often, he is beaten by reality!

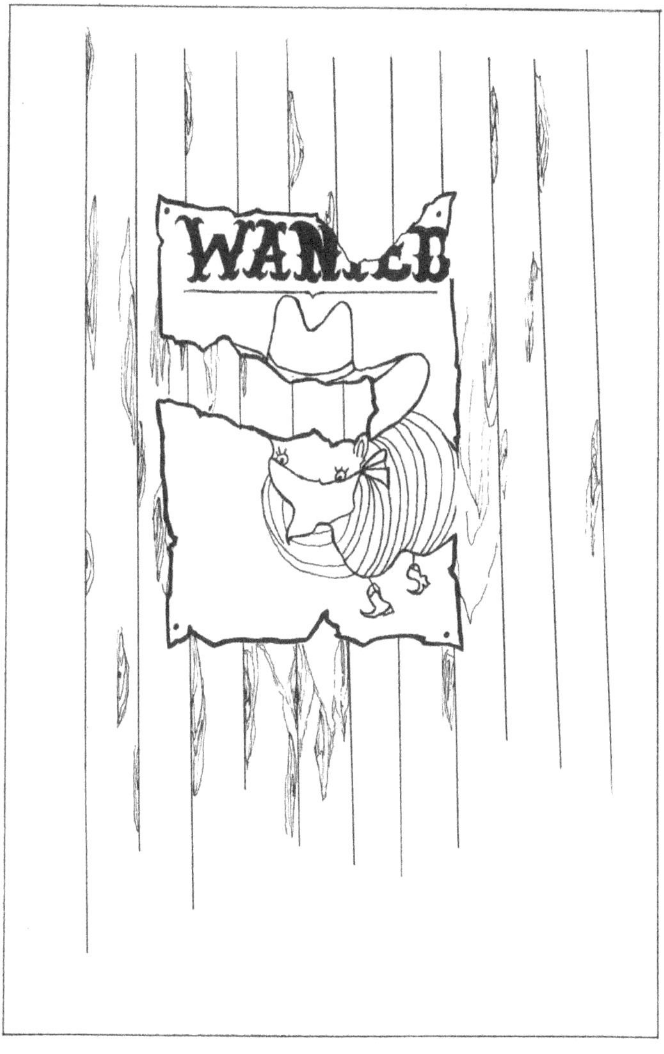

Neighbour Dennis joined them. The elevator still had not come. Dennis, always the trendy one, was already acquainted with virtual hikes. "In fact, I've been working on a virtual drive-through," he explained. "Why burn gas on the highway and suffer in Houston traffic jams! Sit in the car with your family and neighbours, stay in your comfy air-conditioned garage, and my delivery man will come along and serve you! Your satisfaction is guaranteed!"

CHAPTER THE TWENTIETH

IN WHICH WE LEARN SOMETHING IMPORTANT ABOUT THE NATURE OF TEXAS HISTORY

On the next day, the members of the Siblinghood hardly recognised their *consigliere*. Don Pacifico was so broken-hearted that he just sat there gasping and mumbling: "*Non è vero.*" Both his Italian and his Yiddish cunning had failed him. His masterpiece, the jury with a clear majority of felons, had failed him as well. Both Robber Fabio and Chi Ting the Chinese robber girl had been found guilty by the jury.

It took the *consigliere* a lot of effort to find out what had happened in the jury room. But, with the assistance of Robber Igor the debt-collector and Robber Mildred with her notorious handbag, he managed to reveal the ugly truth. Which was that the money forgers had not rallied behind Fabio: they envied him for the superior quality of his products. The perjurers had proven unreliable beyond repair. And the art forgers? They, too, had refused to come to the rescue of Fabio and Chi Ting because they considered money forgery a very inferior part of their business. Creating a fake but unique artefact required so much more skill than just reproducing a standard serigraph, they held. So they all, to their shame it must be said in this true account, sided with the few law-abiding citizens in the jury and returned a verdict of 'guilty'.

The Robber Boss spent more invective on the jury than on the D-town football team in an entire season. Then he asked Robber Jack's PA to collect and analyse data on the gaol's layout, and its escape history. How long would a tunnel have to be, and how many robbers were needed for digging it? What? It was swampland, alligator-infested on top? Near Brazos Bend State Park, oh yes, of course. It would be a frontal attack then? How many guards were there, so how many robbers were needed?

Robber Thyme knew that weapons were not a problem. He had visited the Siblinghood's armoury. Thyme was acquainted with a captain in the German army, whose company, though part of the NATO Response Force, did not have half the firepower of the Siblinghood of Robbers. Still, how many of his robber siblings would be killed in action?

Suddenly, Thyme was inspired to grab the *consigliere* for a tour of the countryside. He had heard from several of his colleagues that, in order to raise one's spirit, there was no better way than to visit Robbers Philemon and Baucis on their farm. They were a couple in their nineties – the oldest and the boldest members of the Siblinghood. They robbed entire houses. Not by going through the house and collecting valuables, as the other robbers would interpret their calling. No, Robbers Philemon and Baucis robbed the house as such. They took the entire structure with them!

The esteemed reader may have seen on the interstate some of these giant trucks that transport complete houses. If it was a house on the register of historic buildings and heading towards La Grange, Texas, chances are that it was one of those robbed by Philemon and Baucis.

Once they had fancied a wooden house in a place called Smithville, Texas which was too large to fit on an 18-wheeler. The couple was undeterred. They had the house chainsawed and the two halves transported separately. The homeowner, who had arrived on the scene just at the climax of the undertaking, very narrowly escaped the lunatic asylum when he tried to report the incident to the police.

On their farm, they had assembled a beautiful collection of historic houses. They filled them with bric-a-brac for ambiance, and commemorated the former owners and their ancestors with neatly polished brass plates.

Philemon and Baucis ran the place as a Non-Profit Organisation, using it for choir retreats, or for meetings of the Texas State Historical Association. Or, like today, as a place where a depressed robber and a disconcerted *consigliere* could watch the sunset, have some German Texan beer, observe the bypassing deer, and recollect their spirits.

And indeed Don Pacifico came back to life. Focusing on that part of his heritage which answered to the name of Reb Shlomo, he made a couple of phone calls to Rice University. It did not take him long to convince the professors of criminal law, Texas history, and Talmudic dialectics that they had no other engagement for tomorrow night. Same with the professor of scholasticism at St Thomas of Aquinas University where, however, the *consigliere* preferred to stress his Italian roots.

Thyme was not part of the meeting that night. He went to celebrate with his Slovak neighbour. Dennis was drunk with joy (and with s*livovitz*, the famous plum brandy of his home region). He had received a higher accolade than any drive-through entrepreneur before him: the city of Houston had decided to change a few of their bus routes, and even the light rail tracks, so that the passengers could benefit from some of Dennis's establishments without having to interrupt their ride.

It has to be noted that planning routes for public transport was a difficult task in Houston. In other cities, real estate prices go up when a neighbourhood gets better connections. Not so in Houston. Homeowners complain that the value of their property will go to the dogs when public transport is directed through their streets. The noise! And the unwelcome sort of people who may come – such as those who don't have a car! So the city was restricted to launching new public transport services only in such areas where the citizens were too lethargic to form an action committee against it.

But this true account needs to go back to Don Pacifico who welcomed his task force of Rice and St Thomas professors at an upscale steak house (no drive-thru this time). There they put their illustrious brains to work, in consequence of which Don Pacifico met with the prison warden, and was able to strike a deal with him.

Convict leasing was the name of the game. True, it had been abolished in Texas more than a hundred years ago. But, in Texas, more than in any other place, the past is never really over. (Texans, though most of them *goyim*, had discovered even before Einstein that time is a relative concept.) So Robbers Fabio and Chi Ting served their prison terms under the auspices of the Siblinghood.

Would they mow the lawn there, sweep the hallways, or wash the robbers' cars? No way. The Siblinghood made much better use of the talents of the two. They were employed in an in-house workshop: in the money forgery. So indeed not much had changed for Fabio and Chi Ting. It was almost back to their old lives, the main difference now being that not only was the Siblinghood's membership fee deducted from their robber's wages, but also the fee that their organisation was charged by the gaol for leasing them out.

True, from time to time they complained that Don Pacifico had not procured a forthright acquittal for them. But the *consigliere* would not listen to this: "*Corpo di Bacco!* If you don't like it here, think of those *trayf* places where they still have chain gangs! *Basta!*"

And look who guarded the two convicts: it was Willie. Willie the police dog. Following the advice of that eternal gentleman, delivered en route from a meeting in Paris and another in Houston before heading off again to Russia, and then to India, Willie had barked his way into the Siblinghood, and been hired by the provost marshal. Wow!

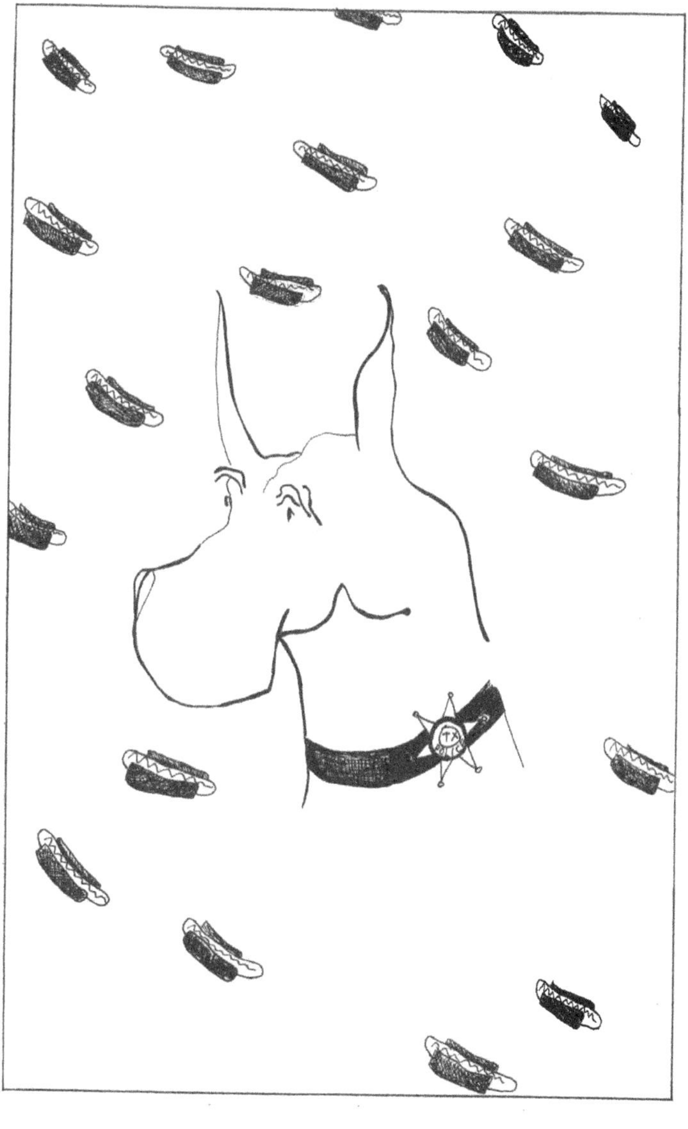

CHAPTER THE TWENTY-FIRST

IN WHICH WE MAKE THE ACQUAINTANCE OF A VERY SPECIAL TOWNSHIP

Not again! But there was no escape. Henny and Rosy, the inseparable twins of HR, had cornered Robber Thyme once more. "Which hairdresser do you go to?" – "Beg parrrdon?" – "Where do you get your hair cut?" – Thyme revealed that he went to a hairdresser who also did Chinese calligraphy. She did his hair very nicely, except on that memorable day when she had been so upset by President Obama's re-election that she had confused the tools of her two trades.

"No good," declared HR. "She's not on the list." They gave him a list of hairdressers appointed, qualified and accredited by the board of directors of the township where he was to rob the next day. "Go to one of them today. Have your boots polished in the morning. And make sure to follow the dress code!"

From the envious looks that the other robbers cast at him from their cubicles, Thyme concluded that it was quite a privilege to be selected for robbery in that area. Take Robber Raoúl for example, or Robber Ezekiel. They had never been allowed to commit as much as a single handbag snatch there. Or Robber Fauxbourdon the Cajun, look at his hair!

The classy people in River Oaks or in the Heights would not mind the occasional weird-looking robber from the Montrose-Westheimer area. They acknowledged that such an encounter enriched their life. But the upstarts in that township North of Beltway 8 feared that their status would be compromised if they admitted non-conformists to their world, even temporarily.

Members of the Siblinghood of Robbers needed a special permit for doing business in said township. Otherwise each one of them would go there almost every day, so attractive was the place due to the affluence of its inhabitants. They could consider themselves lucky that they were admitted at all, for the township had its own Fellowship of Felons, terrible snobs who did not care to have the usual agreements for mutual recognition that the Siblinghood of Robbers had with the other bands of brothers (and sisters, of course) all over the State of Texas and beyond.

The City of Houston had planned to annex the township. But its handpicked inhabitants had had no desire to be amalgamated into Houston's motley population. So they collected and paid a handsome ransom – 16 million dollars! – in order to escape that fate. The *consigliere's* predecessor, Don Clemente, had brokered that deal. Thanks to his intermediation, the Siblinghood was now entitled to two robbery permits per day, to be issued by HR to robbers in good standing, with appropriate haircut and polished boots.

Robber John B was to team up with Thyme. Our hero had donned his best clothes but still felt underdressed when he saw John B's Saville Row outfit. Both of them were rather tired, for they had spent half the night studying the *'Rules and Regulations for Proper Behavior of Non-Residents Occasionally Admitted to our Township through the Undeserved Grace of Its Elected Officers.'* – "And that's nothing compared to the rules for prospective residents," said Robber John B. "Ten volumes! And they have to pass a test on the rules, or they cannot move in!"

The rules included a very strict non-discrimination policy that all prospective residents had to endorse. In result of which policy the township had a population of 80 % whites (by which they mean non-Hispanics, of course), 12 % Hispanics, 5 % Asians, and 2 % blacks.

The Board of Directors of this streamlined, master-planned, perfectionist and guaranteed aseptic community encouraged marriage amongst residents, and promised their descendants a fast-track admission into residency, with the mandatory screening reduced to a minimum, and no quarantine before moving in. The Board's aim was to breed a race of residents who had the rules of behaviour already inherited in their genes. Have we mentioned the name of the place already? Brave New Wood it is called.

So off they went in John B's car, a Land Rover. The Siblinghood's armoury had issued them handguns with silencers, in view of the township's noise control ordinance. They planned to do a few hold-ups near the neat little waterway that ran through the township. In vain they looked for suitable brushwood. Everything was far too nicely trimmed to provide a hideout.

While they were still studying the lay of the land, a policeman approached them. – "A copper?" John B was surprised. "That's not cricket. We haven't even started yet!" – The officer, with chewing gum of an upscale brand in his mouth, studied their permits, their health certificates, and their references. "Nice paperwork," he admitted. "But y'all can't go around robbing here with a beard liked that!" – John B, used his Queen's English to explain that Thyme was a foreign guest robber and thus exempt from the Siblinghood's dress code. Even HR had acknowledged that, in writing. – "Y'all's dress code is your business. Ours is mine. A moustache is all right, but a full beard? No way."

The policeman cast another look at Thyme's permit. "Papers say you're German. So where's your *Lederhose?*" Thyme's explanation about his not being from Bavaria was not well received. His credibility hit rock bottom when he had to admit that he owned neither a Mercedes nor a BMW, not even a Volkswagen. - "Take your Commie-colored beard and get the hell out of here!"

shouted the officer of the peace. "Move!" So their visit to Brave New Wood was over before it had really begun.

Remembering Robber Karl Wilhelm's advice, they drove on to nearby Old Town Spring, a charming little ensemble of well-restored wooden cabins that housed antique and other sorts of shops favoured by affluent customers. The hopelessly overdressed John B with his Queen's English attracted, or rather distracted, an audience of awe-struck elderly gentlemen, enchanted ladies and giggling teenage girls while Thyme collected their watches, jewellery, and purses, never omitting to place his or John B's business card in the pocket he emptied. So a failure was converted into a success, duly celebrated with *Bratwurst* and a couple of German Texan beers at the historic inn of the place.

Based on those business cards, the Chamber of Commerce would later approach the Siblinghood: couldn't they arrange to dispatch some stylish old-world highwaymen to Old Town Spring every weekend? That would further enhance the attractiveness of the place. The Siblinghood was happy to comply, dress code and rules of behaviour to be established before the holiday season. "And in case y'all get a better offer from New Braunfels, we'll match it!" asserted the chairperson of the Chamber.

CHAPTER THE TWENTY-SECOND

IN WHICH ROBBER THYME HAS A NIGHTMARE, AND THIS TRUE ACCOUNT IS MOVING TOWARDS THE END

Robber Thyme was having a nightmare. In his dream, he was on guard duty. It was cold, damp and raining. Fortunately, he woke up. Unfortunately, when he rubbed his eyes, he was still on guard duty, and it was cold, damp and raining very heavily indeed. At least he was not out in the open but sitting in a car, like a private eye in the movies. No Lauren Bacall in sight, though.

In her stead, Robber Mildred appeared on the scene, pointing at her notorious handbag: "I brought you something to drink, pard!" – "Hot coffee, I rrreckon?" inquired Robber Thyme. This being Texas, however, Mildred had brought him ice-cold sodas. Was it Dr. Pepper, the Texan answer to the cultural hegemonists of Atlanta? Yes and no, it was the diet version of it, nicknamed Pepper Paramedic.

"Don't fall asleep, pard!" remarked Robber Mildred casually. "It's crucial that we guard this place! No living soul may enter the house and tamper with the last will, now that the old man may meet his maker at any moment." And off she went in order to relieve Robber Rick who was stationed at the hospice in another part of the same operation.

Robber Thyme knew the background well enough. One of Houston's largest fortunes was at stake. Numerous relatives, ex-wives, mistresses, secretaries, nurses, housekeepers, chauffeurs and gardeners had approached diverse members of the Siblinghood in order to change the content of said will in their favour. Blackmailers and roughnecks, forgers and lawyers had been enlisted to promote the interests of the various parties. The Robber Boss had employed great care to ensure that the Siblinghood members would not work against each other – or, if so, at a premium charge to the prospective heirs, in a coordinated manner, and under safety protocols elaborated by Robber Lennart.

In the end, Don Pacifico, readily supported by an intimidated family lawyer, had taken care of the final and ultimate last will. This sophisticated document, a true masterpiece of criminal diplomacy, duly considered every stakeholder's respective interest and the remuneration he or she had paid for the Siblinghood's service. In a similar manner, several charities had found their way into the testament. A few performing arts companies had come to this honour for free, after Robber Amadeo had hinted to them that it would pay to consider Don Pacifico's eclectic taste (*klezmer* and *verismo*) in their programme planning for the next season.

According to the forecast, the weather would turn even worse. Storms and buckets of rain were predicted. The radio gave long lists of schools and government offices that would remain closed tomorrow. Thyme's mood did not improve when he heard that the theatre performance for which he and Dr Matasano had tickets was cancelled as well. Shakespeare's 'Tempest,' called off because of a storm? "If they are scarrred to death of the weatherrr herrre, they ought to rrreturrrn the place to the Mexicans!" thundered Thyme. Although he doubted very much that even Robber Raoúl would endorse that.

At midnight Robber Fabio came to relieve Thyme. The convict, guarded by Willie, had to take the ever unpopular dog-watch. Thyme reported that nothing remarkable had occurred during his watch. No message from the hospice, and no movements here. Only the elderly gentleman with the goatee beard had passed in a cab. Thyme had heard him arguing with the cab driver. All flights in and out of Houston were cancelled due to the foul weather? "If that is so, young man, take me to the bus terminal."

"Why can't he stay put until the storrrm is overrr?" wondered Robber Thyme. – "¿Stay put? No, he can't do that," retorted Robber Fabio. "Of all people in the world, he's the one who can't do that … until Kingdom come." – Thyme looked puzzled. – "The Hispanic waitstaff all over town knows who he is." Fabio continued. "¿You still don't?. You should … I suspect you're Lutheran, no offence … but even so you should recognise that gentleman." Fabio checked his watch. "Listen, your shift is over. Do some reading before you hit the hay tonight." He shook his head: "¿C'mon, have you never heard of Ahasver the Wandering Jew?"

Back in his apartment and a short but intense Internet research later, Thyme could not sleep. Throughout the night and the following day he thought with pity on the wandering gentleman. How he had refused rest to Jesus on His way to crucifixion, and was now cursed to restlessly roam the world until Christ would return.

Thyme himself had rather the opposite fate today: he wanted to get moving, but he could not. The weather was too bad to do any outside work, and the office of the Siblinghood was closed for the same reason. In a gloomy mood, Thyme watched TV reports about streets flooded and buildings destroyed. Lucky were the robbers who did Internet fraud from their home office – at least until a power failure put them out of business for a day or more.

"We need a business model that makes us less dependent on the weather," Robber Thyme, by now slightly sneezing, told his Slovak neighbour. For the Internet fraudsters, it was easy: just give them uninterrupted power supplies and satellite communication. But weather-proof hold-ups and burglaries were more difficult to arrange. Dennis promised to think about it.

In the evening the storm was over. The following day brought the robbers back to their cubicles at the Siblinghood. Robber Thyme visited Robber Fabio at the money-printing workshop. He needed to talk about Ahasver the Wandering Jew.

Thyme told Fabio how Ahasver once had pronounced: "I know why I keep moving all the time, but why are all the others?" – "That's the point, exactly. Think about this: I see him as Christ's brother," declared Robber Fabio the sideline theologian, "a brother in fate. Ahasver has taken the curse of restlessness upon himself on behalf of all mankind. But we all keep moving, running, rushing – all the time, from one place to the next. Same with Christ. Most of us humans, we just don't behave as if we had been saved."

"¡I've got an idea!" Unnoticed by the two of them, Amanda the Sassy Armadillo had overheard their conversation. And so, when Ahasver was in town again, the three of them, plus Dennis the Slovak and Dr Matasano, grabbed him and took him to a high-rise building that sported a revolving restaurant. Dennis of course immediately imagined a high-rise building with an elevator for cars and a revolving drive-through restaurant on the highest floor.

"¿Revolving, you see?" Amanda brought them back to the here and now. "¡It's moving all the time! ¡So you can sit still as long as you please, baby!" – The Wandering Jew needed a while to recover from this form of address. When he had last been called baby, Emperor Augustus was still sitting on his throne in Rome. "You're not only a Southern belle, you're a smart young lady!" he responded at last. Now it was Amanda who had to recover from this form of address. And Ahasver was able to enjoy his dinner most thoroughly, eating five courses, having all the time in the world.

CHAPTER THE LAST

IN WHICH THIS TRUE ACCOUNT COMES TO AN END

Thyme talked with a few other robbers at the Siblinghood. He was curious how they perceived the Wandering Jew. Don Pacifico the *consigliere* complained that Jesus had cursed a simple shoemaker, not a lawyer. Imagine if he could discuss the most famous law cases of the past two millennia with an eyewitness versed in the law!

Robber Fauxbourdon did not understand why they would see Ahasver so frequently: "Why 'oustón, if 'e 'as the 'ole world to roam?" – "Must be the oil & gas business, buddy," Robber Rob was convinced. "He as a Jew, looking at all those Arabs with their oil …" – "Or he has an investment in the Texas Medical Center," Robber Mildred speculated. – "Let's not forrrget he's a shoemakerrr, and has his tools with him" remarked Robber Thyme.

Robber Jack wanted to know whether Ahasver had met the Flying Dutchman out there on the seven seas. His PA planned to tap Ahasver's first-hand knowledge of history to design some more business schemes: *'Esteemed Clients! Enjoy your personal robbery experience (your choice!) in Robin Hood fashion, in baroque style, or in the authentic mode of the Imperial Roman highwaymen.'*

The following day, however, the robbers did not ponder upon Ahasver at all. In fact, they were most agitated: the Kingpin had arrived in Houston, the *capo di tutti i capi*. In the flesh, not via video message. The Robber Boss was said to be having off-site conferences with him, with the *consigliere* and with HR. Nobody knew the meaning of all of this. The Siblinghood was humming like a beehive. Rumours and counterrumours buzzed through the hallways. Denials and disclaimers were issued by the dozen but nobody believed them.

What was being deliberated behind those closed doors? – "A new *modus operandi* for Hobby Airport, now that it will be opened for international flights," Phil the felon and Airport Eddy ventured out. – "A new captain will come aboard," Robber Jack was convinced. – "Another reorganisation," several others believed. – "The Last Judgement," Robber Ezekiel put it. – "An unfriendly takeover," Jack's PA suspected.

Some robbers with many years of service smelled an incentive for early retirement. Others thought that in these unruly times the Siblinghood should offer a retention bonus, so that the key people would stay on board instead of joining the competition. Various robbers called both of these notions wishful thinking. In one way or another, every single robber was disconcerted.

And it got worse. Willie the police dog was suspected as a spy or stool pigeon. He took offence, but soon realised that every Tom, Dick and Harry within the Siblinghood was the subject of slanders and allegations, from the rank and file up to the top brass. The Provost Marshal – hadn't he been seen fishing and hunting with the lieutenant of Company 'A' Texas Rangers? The Robber Boss himself had been seen flirting with the Mayor of Houston. No, others insisted, she (the Mayor) had not been kissed by the Robber Boss but by Robber Mildred.

Many robbers claimed to have it straight from the horse's mouth that new Key Performance Indicators would be introduced at the Siblinghood. To some it had transpired that revenue per mile would be the KPI of the future: how much booty would a robber bring home for every mile of driving to the jobsite. An important consideration given the notorious Houston traffic! The Internet fraudsters rejoiced at that prospect – until Robber Q told them he would measure the mileage of every electron on the World Wide Web.

According to other pieces of scuttlebutt, the business model of the Siblinghood would be drastically altered, with job losses being the inevitable consequence. No more street robberies, just threatening calls from a call centre on the other side of the globe, or from a Native Americans' reservation. No more burglaries, except by robots. It was an open secret that Robber Q, supported by a few kids from Texas ATM University, was working on an ARM, an Automated Robbing Machine. The first prototype was known to have been destroyed by a short circuit in an encounter with an electric guard dog. But since then the project had surely made significant progress.

Only the robbers in the Siblinghood's central departments remained calm. It was in their DNA that they would never be affected by headcount reductions. Whatever cost cutting measures were introduced, rigorous monitoring and a sound reporting scheme would be required during all phases of execution. Thus all central department staff was convinced they had a job guarantee. Little did they know about the outsourcing and robotisation studies that the Kingpin himself had commissioned for their very own tasks.

"That unfrrriendly takeoverrr you werrre talking about," Robber Thyme inquired of Robber Jack's PA, "d'you mean the copperrrs will do a rrrazzia?" – "No, sir," was the answer. "You are certainly aware of the paramount importance of mergers and acquisitions in today's corporate world? We are part of it." – "How's that? I thought the Siblinghood was rrratherrr a guild, orrr a cooperrrative society." – "No, sir, we're a regular business. A franchise. So is the police, by the way."

For the other robbers this was a well-known fact, as their indifferent reactions showed. At most they speculated who might be amongst their shareholders: some hedge funds, Warren Buffett, the Government of Singapore Investment Corporation, or perhaps a Russian oligarch? Maybe a Chinese tycoon, with Chi Ting the robber girl as the advance party? Or some venture capitalists from

Israel, wouldn't that explain the frequent appearances of Ahasver?

For Robber Thyme and his old world background, this franchise thing was a hard nut to crack. He needed to find out more about it. – "We not only have rules of conduct as a big corporation," the PA drove on relentlessly. "We are part of the corporate world." – "Thunderrr and Dorrria! But who would attempt such a takeoverrr? A rrrival gang? The Mexican carrrtels? Orrr the trrriads? No discrrrimination," he added automatically. – "The usual suspects, sir," the PA replied, "but we need to think big. What do we offer to our clientele?" he asked rhetorically. "Empty pockets and a world-class service, yes, you bet. But there is much more to it, sir. Think of Robber Raoúl when he rides as Zorro. Or those ladies of yours with their coffee party. We offer excitement. Adrenaline. Meaning in life. A once-in-a-lifetime experience, every time anew!"

Now the other robbers had formed a circle around Robber Jack's PA, digesting his words of wisdom. "So, who are our competitors in this business?" The PA made a dramatic pause. "Have y'all been to Orlando?" – "Sure we have!" – "Taken the kids there." – "Plenty of times!"

"It is the mission of our Siblinghood to provide excitement, just as a theme park does. Theme parks, computer gaming, our activities … it's all overlapping. We will be bought by one of the big theme parks sooner or later. They will not tolerate us robbers giving people excitement outside the sphere of their theme park industry. But don't you worry, our business will only gain from this. There will be multifarious synergies. And our customers will benefit beyond their wildest expectations."

Robber Thyme was eager to know where all this would lead. At his request, his Robbers' Guild back home in Germany agreed with the Siblinghood to extend Thyme's delegation. The first-hand experience he was about to gain in the breakthrough developments in Houston would be invaluable for the future of robbery in his home town.

Nevertheless, Thyme was a bit melancholic: "The worrrld as we know it will turrrn into a giant theme parrrk!" – "Yes, it will!" The PA was enthusiastic about it. "In fact, we are already halfway there!"

Thyme discussed these prospects with his neighbours. Dr Matasano was not surprised. His own profession, with childbirth and surgery as reality shows live on TV, had already gone in the same direction. "¡Don't tilt at windmills, my friend!" was his advice. – "I'll trrry not to," retorted Thyme melancholically, "but if I do, I'll post it on Twitter!"

Dennis shared the doctor's opinion. His businesses benefitted a lot from the lifestyle of the modern world. "Back home in the olden days, as they are calling them ... what would I have been? A bonded peasant!"

The next day Thyme asked Robber Fabio what he thought about this theme park notion. – "Not at all a new notion, this one," stated Fabio the sideline philosopher. "¿Did it never occur to you? ¡The whole world's a stage!"

Thyme tried to make his peace with the theme park notion. Over dinner at Dennis' Drive-Thru Dutch Pancakes, they were united in praising Amanda for having taken Ahasver to the revolving restaurant where he could take a rest from early evening until closing time. – And there arrived Ahasver himself, nodding to the robbers, but obviously in a dark and gloomy mood. "They refused my application," he responded to Thyme's inquiry. "I am welcome in my supporting capacity as a lobbyist and venture capital broker, they say, but will have no active part in the mission. No shoemakers needed, they claim. And I don't have enough experience, they say! As if I were too young, I of all people. I've tried with NASA here, with the Europeans in Paris, even with the Russians and Indians. No ticket to Mars for me."

"To Marrrs? Why would you want to go therrre?" Robber Thyme demanded to know. "A new starrrt forrr mankind, you think?" – "I don't expect that much," retorted Ahasver. "I lost my illusions many centuries ago … when Emperor Titus destroyed the Temple at Jerusalem. And you know my condition. Even in a Mars colony I couldn't settle down. No, I'm a practical man, looking for a little bit of comfort in my constant travels. Being on board a spaceship for ever so many months, doesn't that sound a lot better than having to rush for another plane at least twice a day? Even better than the Trans-Siberian Railway!"

"I understand you must be always on the move," exclaimed Dennis the Slovak. "Well, I believe I've got something for you, right here and now! Remember my Drive-Thru Dormitory? Where the students live in cars on a conveyer? C'mon, my eternal friend, go ahead and rent a stretch limo …" – "Or even an RV," Dr Matasano threw in. – "Right, sawbones! Place it on my conveyer, and have a good rest while still in motion for however long you want!"

Ahasver was thrilled by this proposal and asked Dennis to reserve a comfy space for him. Robber Thyme had to admit that, seen from this perspective, modern times had their advantages, even if you were such an archaic figure as Ahasver.

"And we'll find something for you as well," Dennis promised. "Robber Jack has arranged that his PA will give me a hand when I develop a business model for you." – Thyme reminded Dennis that the personal element was crucial for his way of work. The live encounter. The human interface, as the PA would probably call it. Especially in Houston with its friendly population. Dennis assured Thyme he would pay due attention to this aspect.

And he was as good as his word. Two short months later, Robber Thyme was no longer obliged to roam streets and back yards in the glaring heat, or in the pouring rain. He sat behind a counter to which a grateful clientele flocked in their pick-ups with the precision of clockwork. Dependent on their level of liquidity, the esteemed clientele could first visit an ATM, a pawnbroker, or a loan shark before approaching Thyme at his counter, all of this without leaving their car. And it was so convenient that everything was co-located!

'Dennis' Drive-Thru Daylight Robbery' said the sign above, 'Open 24/7. Satisfaction guaranteed.' Robber Jack's PA waved at Thyme as he passed by in his brand-new pick-up. Ildefons the Iguana sat smiling on Thyme's shoulder, taking turns with Amanda the Armadillo. And Benedict the Earthworm had promised to visit Houston soon.

THE AUTHOR & THE ILLUSTRATOR

With open eyes for both the beautiful and the absurd in everyday life, **Marec Béla Steffens** (from Hamburg, Germany) and his wife and illustrator **Krystyna** (who grew up in Warsaw, Poland) have lived in several countries – including two stints in Houston; the more recent one in 2012-16. This is their sixth book (not counting his PhD thesis in economics), and the first one in English. The previous books were all in German; this book is published in German as *Thymian in Texas* by Geest-Verlag.

Marec is also working as a librettist for composers Mary Carol Warwick (on Spanish governor Bernardo de Gálvez and his crucial contribution to American independence), his father Walter Steffens, Mario Wiegand and Clare Glackin, with performances in Houston and Round Top, Texas; London, UK (Sadler's Wells); Rheinsberg and Kassel, Germany.

Contact: maerchenkater@web.de

Marec's website: www.maerchenkater.de

Krystyna's website: www.krystynasteffens.de

The German publisher: www.geest-verlag.de

Back cover photo: Chuck Alexander

In the previous book, *Der Räuber Thymian*, Robber Thyme lived and robbed in peace in his German hometown …